THE
BELLS
OF TIMES
SQUARE

AMY LANE

RIPTIDE
PUBLISHING

Riptide Publishing
PO Box 6652
Hillsborough, NJ 08844
www.riptidepublishing.com

The Bells of Times Square

Cover Art by Reese Dante, http://www.reesedante.com
Editors: Sarah Frantz and Danielle Poiesz
Layout: L.C. Chase, http://lcchase.com/design.htm

ISBN: 978-1-62649-186-1

First edition
December 2014

Also available in ebook:
ISBN: 978-1-62649-185-4

THE BELLS OF TIMES SQUARE

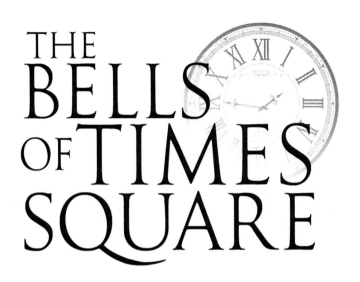

AMY LANE

RIPTIDE
PUBLISHING

TABLE OF CONTENTS

DAWN OF A NEW AGE

"Mom, is he ready?"

If Nate Meyer could have smiled, he would have, but his face didn't do that anymore.

"Blaine, honey, it's freezing outside. Really? Are we really doing this?"

Nate closed his rheumy eyes. His wrinkled, liver-spotted hand shimmied as he plucked at the polyester blanket across his lap. *Please, Stephanie. Please. The bells. I might hear the bells.*

"Mom, he lives for this, you know that."

Good boy. Blaine, such a good boy. Dark black hair, big brown eyes—couldn't look more like me as a young man if we'd tried.

But then, Stephanie had married a nice boy, a dentist, with black hair and brown eyes as well, and she'd laughed about that. A good Jewish girl marrying a Jewish dentist—it was like she'd read a manual, yes? Her children would look almost *frum*. Nate and Carmen had laughed quietly about that as well, because Stephanie herself looked German. Her brother Alan had blond hair and brown eyes, although Nate suspected that after he hit twenty-five, the blond streaks had come from a bottle. Well, yes, a man could do that now, in these days. A man could dye his hair and not be accused of being a . . . What had Walter called them?

Poof. Yes, that was the word.

A man could streak his hair and dress himself fancy, and not be afraid of being a poof.

In his head, Nate laughed, and he could see himself as Walter had seen him: just like Blaine with his dark curly hair, dark-brown eyes, dark lashes, full lips, a slight space between his teeth, and a nose with a decided bow outwards. He'd always looked like a Jew, had never been ashamed of it, not even when he'd moved from his predominantly Jewish neighborhood in the Lower East Side to the barracks with the other USAAF privates, some of them from places in the country that had never seen a Jew before. That posting hadn't lasted long, though.

Somewhere, somebody had seen his recruitment papers. The degree in art history meant nothing, but his father was a clockmaker, and Nate worked in his shop. His specialty? Cameras, the new and the old. And Nathan Meyer suddenly became a valuable commodity, didn't he? Six-pointed star and all, Nate could work cameras, and in 1941, when Brits had just started figuring out how to outfit their Spitfires so the pilots didn't die and the cameras didn't freeze, that man who could take a picture was like gold, wasn't he?

Nate hadn't hidden his gloating, either, when he'd been recruited by the OSS while in the USAAF. He'd been inducted into the 25th Tactical and Reconnaissance Wing—more specifically, the 654th bombardment. Him, Nate Meyer. Even *he* had something special, something the OSS needed.

It had started with the clocks. Everyone had something to contribute, because that was the war, right? Even Nate's mother had planted a victory garden in the flower bed she kept in the little concrete apron behind the family brownstone. Before the crash, when Nate was a little boy, she'd worn gloves when dusting to keep her hands soft. And now, with the crash and the war? She was gardening!

And Nate, who had needed to beg his father to buy an old Brownie and then had taken it apart, put it together, learned all the words—f-stop, shutter speed, lens width, scope—while his father complained bitterly about the newfangled thing and the expense of the invention, *that* Nate now had a special skill to offer. So he got the promotion and the raise in pay and the better bunk, and all for taking pictures.

His father hadn't been so proud. *Pictures? What good were pictures? Officers needed pictures; the war needed* men! But of course, pictures of officers were what Nate had told his parents he took so his letters home didn't look like a picture puzzle. In reality, his pictures were very different . . .

"Grandpa? Are you ready yet?"

Not so ready. Because my body is meat, boy, and no amount of wiping it off or swaddling it in these acrylic afghans your mother makes will render it more than meat.

Blaine didn't hear him, of course. He was a strong boy, and Nate had enough of himself to wrap his arms around Blaine's neck so the boy could lift him up from his bed and set him in his wheelchair. Stephanie's husband—another good boy. Oh, Nate was surrounded by good boys. He was grateful—had a ramp installed. So thank heavens, there would be no *bump-kerthump, bump-kerthump*, as there had been so often in the first days after the stroke.

"Mom! Where's his coat? The thick wool one, with the leather gloves in the pocket?"

"Blaine, do you really want to—"

There was a knock at the front, and Stephanie left off her nagging, probably to open the door.

"That's Tony," Blaine said. He had always liked talking to Nate and had kept up the habit of it even after Nate couldn't talk anymore. Nate might find it irritating as hell, but at least Blaine talked about real things. He certainly could do without Stephanie's yammering about buying something new for the house. He hated the new things—the new tile, the new tables—because her mother had worked so hard for the old things. It felt disloyal, this opening of the house, the sunshiny colors, the skylight over the living room. Hearing Stephanie justify these things to Nate—that only hurt him more.

But Blaine talked about politics, he talked about books.

And because Nate couldn't talk, couldn't tell, couldn't condemn, Blaine also talked about Tony.

Nate lived for Blaine's monologues about Tony.

At first it had been Tony's mind—the funny things that Tony had said. Tony was in Blaine's sociology course at NYU, and he had the best things, the best shows, the best songs.

Then it had been Tony's laughter, the jokes that he told and how he liked action-adventure movies and didn't like the Oscar ones because they were too sad. Blaine had been disappointed by this at first, because Blaine himself was always so serious, always so worried about tomorrow. But Nate had listened, and Blaine had started to laugh at himself more, appreciate that you needed to laugh in order to work toward a better tomorrow.

Sometimes Blaine would talk about how he'd been giving Tony lessons about being a Jew, which made Nate laugh inside. When *Nate* had been Blaine's age, he hadn't even spoken Yiddish in an attempt to not align himself with his father or any of the traditions that Nate had been forced to follow, simply because they *were* traditions. He had changed when he'd come home from the war, embraced those stories, loved those traditions, for Carmen's sake, for his own, for his family's.

And Blaine had learned to love them as well. Blaine would study the Passover Seder stories and the Purim stories, and tell them to Tony, and then come home and tell his *zayde* all about Tony's reactions. So yes, Nate had heard all about Tony's love of a good story.

More recently, he'd heard all about Tony's smile.

But Nate had yet to meet Tony, and now, hearing the suppressed excitement in Blaine's voice, he was suddenly excited, as well. He was going out, out into the cold to listen for the bells, and he would get to meet Blaine's Tony. He made an effort then, worked hard, and a sound came out. A happy sound, he hoped.

"You like that?" Blaine smiled while he helped Nate into his coat. "You want to meet Tony? He'll like you. I told him you were a hero in the war, you know? He thought that was pretty awesome."

Awesome—everything these days was *awesome* or *excellent* or *wonderful*. What about Blaine's generation made them talk in superlatives? Nate missed the days when you could understate things, when it would be *nice* or *nifty* or *interesting* instead.

Of course, if Nate had lived in a time when your whole life could be accomplished on a little glowing box on the kitchen table, well then, everything might indeed have been awesome, wouldn't it?

But Blaine didn't hear Nate's thoughts on *awesome*.

"I wanted him to meet you. I mean, I know you can't exactly tell him stories, *Zayde*, but you know . . ."

You wanted to know if I would welcome him, love him as you do already. You wanted to know if Zayde *would bless you and make it all good, even if your mother would say to stop this* mishegas *already, there is no gay in her family.*

The moment stretched on achingly as Blaine helped him with his gloves. Nate remembered this boy when he was a child. He would cling to Nate's hand, bury his face in Nate's thick wool coat whenever they went outdoors during the holidays. New York, even the Upper East Side, was loud and frightening for a small boy. And now, the boy had found another hand to help him through, and he wanted to know if his *Zayde* would bind their hands together, like a rabbi at a wedding.

Nate longed to give his blessing.

Blaine buttoned up Nate's coat. He was sweltering inside it, but, well, it was better than freezing as soon as they made it outside. Blaine was in the middle of tucking another blanket around Nate's lap when he turned.

"Tony!" The warmth of his voice, the pitch of the enthusiasm, told Nate far too much about how hard it was to be here, wrapping his grandfather up like a swaddled child, to help him honor this old tradition.

"Is he all ready?" Tony asked cheerfully, and Nate's good eye focused on him.

Oh my. The left side of his face could still move, and he knew he was smiling in pleased surprise.

Tony was a handsome boy, with skin nearly the color of Nate's black wool coat and teeth that gleamed against that dark skin. *Oh, look at them!* Boys who could look at each other and smile like that, dark skin and six-pointed star and all.

If Nate could have spoken, he would have said *Awesome!* or *Excellent!*

Blaine . . . such a good boy.

Of course, Nate's father would have said no such thing about Blaine's choice. But then Selig Meyer had not been a fan of Carmen when she had first followed Nate home from the library in the fall of '47—although he'd never said so to her face. Too fair, too blue eyed, too delicate, even though her parents went to the same temple as Nate's family, when his father went at all. But he'd come to love her—probably more than he loved his only son—by the end.

A boy—any boy, no less a boy like this one—would have sent Nate running from the city, his father's outraged disappointment chasing him like a black wave.

But then, no boy had ever really appealed to Nate after Provence Claire La Lune. No girl, either, but Carmen had been kind, and determined. A marriage—a kosher marriage—had been no less than her ultimate goal, and Nate, so lost after the war, what was he to do?

"Hereyago, Mr. Meyer!" Tony was right behind him, pushing the chair down the ramp, holding the back of it so very low to keep it from pitching. "Blaine's been looking forward to this for a week, you know. Kept trying to tell me about the bells."

Nate glanced around, his right eye rolling frantically in the useless, drooping side of his face. He made a noise then, a panicked and inarticulate noise, because—

"Blaine's back in the house, Mr. Meyer," Tony said quickly. "No worries. You got no worries at all. He was just checking with his mom. Didn't want her to panic none, 'cause he said he was going to edge in close to 37th Street tonight, and it's a bit of a walk, and sort of a riot, but you know that."

Nate let out a long exhale, and the slap of the wind tried to steal that breath from him as it went. Of course, of course. Blaine would not leave him in the hands of someone who would not care for him. That was not his way.

"You ready?" Blaine called from the top of the stairs. "Ready, Grandpa? We're going to stop down at the corner for some hot chocolate, and then make our way toward Times Square."

"Man, that place is gonna be crowded. Do you really wanna go all that way?"

Nate couldn't be sure, but he thought there might have been a touch of . . . something. There was a pause that bespoke intimacy, of that he was certain.

"We're not going all the way into the square," Blaine said quietly. "We're going *near* the square. Close enough to hear church bells, if there are any."

"Church bells," Tony said blankly. "I know you told me this, but why are we listening for church bells again? Do church bells even *ring* on New Year's at Times Square?"

I don't know, Nate thought. *I never heard them.*

"And besides, aren't you Jewish?"

Blaine laughed shyly. "You really have to ask?"

Tony's return laugh was fond. "No, I guess not. So why church bells? Why not temple bells or something?"

Blaine sighed. "I'm not really sure. It's just . . . It's weird, really. Grandpa, for as long as I can remember, he's gone on a walk on New Year's Eve—Mom said he did it when she was little too. Grandma never went. He always said he was listening for bells."

Once. My Carmen went once. Then she gave the walk to me, my once a year, to listen for church bells.

"That's sort of cool," Tony said, and Nate could feel his regard. For a moment, Nate was the handsome, strapping man who had gone off to war, and he was confused. Wasn't he wounded, slight, limping on the damaged body that kept him from returning to active duty, the lone stranger in any crowd? Older, seasoned, a child on his hip and one by the hand? Middle-aged, successful, a hard-working photographer with his own exclusive Manhattan boutique?

Old, bereft, a widower, remembering how to make his own toast and the reasons a man should get out of bed in the morning?

Helpless, afloat in his own head, his body a lingering wreck of lung sounds and heartbeats, his only power in his thrice-weekly visits to the pool with an aqua teacher?

Young and in love, holding his male lover to his chest after the fury of the *mishkav zakhar*, the one act between men that was considered unforgivable, that reshaped the hearts of them both.

Oh God, the merciful and wise, who *was* Nathan Selig Meyer, and where was he in time?

The distant sound of shouts called him to the present, the faraway merriment reminding him that those shouts of joy were just out of his reach.

Walter, are you there? Are they ringing the bells? I can't hear the bells!

"Here we go, Grandpa," Blaine said, pulling the wheelchair back next to a bench. They were in a lovely neighborhood, not too far from the statue of the tailor and the needle. He used to see stage actors here, sometimes. Nate didn't know if they owned or rented, but he loved the excitement of walking down the street and, Hey! There was someone you'd seen perpetrate magic on the stage or the screen.

He enjoyed this place, this bench under the tree. Blaine had chosen well.

He could hear Blaine and Tony sitting down on the bench beside him, talking animatedly, in a way that bespoke great familiarity.

"So, we're out here to hear bells that don't get rung?" Tony sounded skeptical, but playful too.

"Yeah," Blaine replied shyly. "I mean, I looked it up once. The most I could get was a reference, mind you, that a nearby church rang bells on New Year's Eve during the war."

"Did you keep it?"

"Are you kidding? You've seen me study!"

Tony made an exasperated sound. "Augh, kid, you are *killing* me. You know I live for this stuff."

"I'm a year younger than you, smart-ass, but look here. I brought you something."

Nate saw Blaine pull something out of his coat, and inside, he smiled.

"Oh wow! A scrapbook!"

"Yeah, apparently my great-grandmother kept a scrapbook of *Zayde*—"

"Thereyago, talking Jewish to me again!"

Blaine laughed, but it wasn't embarrassed. "Yiddish, Tony. We call it Yiddish, and I only know a few words. It's like 'Grandpa,' but, you know, affectionate, like 'Papa' or 'Grampy'—*Zayde*."

A speculative silence then. "*Zayde* . . . That's nice. What about, you know . . ." And now Tony was the shy one. "What I want to call you, but nothing sounds right."

"Mmm." Blaine's voice fell, then rose intimately. "*Tateleh*, I think."

Tony laughed a little. "That don't hardly sound real. But, you know, better than 'baby.'"

"*Oy gevalt*!" Blaine exaggerated, and they both laughed again, the sound low and personal. "*Anything's* better than 'baby'!"

More laughter, and instead of feeling excluded, Nate felt the opposite. Like he was in on the joke, in on the secret. He knew something about these two young men that nobody else did.

"Seriously," Tony said, the laughter in his voice faded and sad. "You got all these traditions—"

"Not so many, now," Blaine said quickly. "My grandparents, they were Reformed Jews—sort of like, modern but, you know, you gotta say it different. I'm not sure if *Zayde* believed, exactly, but he thought it was important. Traditions were important to him—us belonging somewhere. He said that a lot to my mom, that we needed a chance to belong. He wanted that. But"—and Nate could imagine Blaine's shrug—"my parents, they barely made it to temple."

"You got a bar mitzvah, though," Tony chided.

Blaine grunted. Direct hit. "It was a party, you know? I said some verses, recited some Torah, got the party. Mom didn't want her neighbors to think we couldn't afford it; it was a status thing."

"But you liked the words. You told me that. The words mean something to you."

"Yeah, but only the good ones. Why is this important, anyway?"

It was Tony's turn to grunt, and Nate couldn't see, couldn't turn his head, but he heard what sounded like a kiss. On the cheek, on the hand, on the lips, Nate couldn't be sure, but men, they didn't sit and kiss parts of each other when they were talking about sports or the weather.

"Because it is," Tony said lowly. "I want to look at your family scrapbook and say, 'Hey! That's my boyfriend's history!' Is that so bad?"

"No." There were more kissing sounds, and Nate burned inside to talk to them, to tell them, to explain. The Orthodox rabbis said one thing and the Reformed rabbis said another. It was supposed to be okay if you were *that way*, as long as you didn't act on it, but Nate had been young, he'd felt the pull, the strength like steel springs, binding a human heart to another. What was talk of an unseen God when the world had fallen to chaos? All was hell and violence—how bad could the *mishkav zakhar* be?

"Does your mom know?" Blaine asked when the kissing sounds stopped. "Did you tell her?"

"About you? No."

Blaine grunted shortly, but it sounded hurt, not angry.

"You need to be ready to come out to *your* family first, you know that right?" Tony said sternly, and it must have been an argument they'd had before, because Blaine's sound changed.

He sighed instead. In Nate's line of vision, a parade of cars trolled slowly down the street, headlamps slicing through the darkness like the wind was currently slicing through Nate's coat. Light, steel, it all found a way in.

"But my mom knows about me," Tony said, sighing. "I told you that. When I was a little kid, I said I liked boys. She cried, she tried to talk me out of it, she threatened to have my uncle beat the gay out of me. But Uncle Jason wouldn't do it, and in the end, she just accepted it. I just had to be . . . you know . . ."

"Stubborn," Blaine said. "You."

Nate wanted to see them. More cars wandered the night, but in his mind, he saw that beautiful young man with the skin like night touching Blaine's hair, his forehead, his cheek. Tenderness, Nate imagined. There would be tenderness.

Abruptly, his skin—which had deadened, had become blind to the realm of touch—ached for tenderness like amputees were said to ache for missing limbs. Once, Nate had known such tenderness, and he would never feel it again, not in this body.

"Would they cut you off?" Tony asked. "If you came out? If we moved in, like we've been talking about?"

"Eh . . ." Blaine said uncertainly. "I don't know." Nate heard rustling, and from his finite line of vision, he saw Blaine's knees shift so the boy was facing Nate. "I don't think Grandpa would, even with all the tradition, because . . . I don't know. Because he was just too good a guy. But my mom, well . . ." He grunted. "I heard my grandpa call her *kalta neshomeh* once, when she was redecorating the house after Grandma died. He was hurt, you know? I mean, she said he was just being cheap because, well, I guess it was a thing. The Depression had everybody saving money and stuff, but it was more than that— All of Grandma's stuff was getting put in storage and sold, and Grandpa was shoved into a room and . . . and it wasn't right."

"So what does it mean?"

"I had to ask our rabbi. I think he yelled at Grandpa for it too. It means 'cold soul.'"

Tony's low whistle made Nate smile inside. *Oh yes, yes I did call her that. She deserved it, selling her mother's things like that. No, we did not go to temple as often as we could have, but we had a happy home. Those things should not have been sold as if they had no meaning.* Carmen's old jewelry boxes, her costume jewelry, the desk where she'd done the store and family accounts for more than forty years. Couldn't Stephanie have waited until Nate died? It wasn't like he had more time than anyone else! Of course, Nate chuckled inwardly, that had been six years ago, and he was still hanging around. Perhaps he *did* have more time!

"Wow," Tony said in the resulting quiet. Then, low voiced, urgent: "I have my own apartment. You have a job working at the hospital. I mean, we've talked about it before, but even if they cut you off, you could move in anyway. You *know* I want you with me, right?"

"I want to be there too," Blaine said plaintively. "But my mother—"

"I mean, you could still be a doctor, even if your mother doesn't want to pay for school. You'd have to take out loans and stuff, but, it's like, people are always so afraid of not having any money, but whether you have it or not, you're living your life, and that's the fun part, right? If you've got food, a roof over your head—"

He was so urgent, so upset. Nate wanted to reassure him. *He loves you, Tony. Don't worry. Our boy will do the right thing.*

"*Sha shtil, tateleh,*" Blaine said, and his knees shifted in Nate's vision again. Nate could picture them, Blaine holding Tony so that his face buried into Blaine's deceptively wide shoulder, their faces close together, a dropped kiss on Tony's forehead. "I hear you."

"Yeah, well, you don't have anything to say to me!" There was a rustle, and Tony must have stood up because so did Blaine. Nate gave up chasing cars in the darkness. He closed his eyes and saw the boys—his boys—like a movie.

Oh, Walter. It looks like a good one. A romance—I wonder how it ends.

"I want to say yes," Blaine murmured. "But I need to ask *Zayde*."

"You need to ask—"

Yes, bubeleh, *I am confused, as well.*

"Don't say it," Blaine told him softly. "I just . . . I want so badly to talk to someone in my family, do you understand? He's the one person who told me about tradition and about banding together with people who care about you, and he's the one person who can't say he doesn't love me anymore."

"I hear you." An ironic pause. "Bells, huh?"

"Yes. I am not so sure we will hear any tonight, but if we do, maybe we should take it as a sign, you think?"

"I think I'm freezing my ass off, that's what I think. You said coffee?"

"Thank you. See it? Three blocks up."

"Yeah, I know. Is your gramps gonna want some?"

"Get him hot chocolate—me too, for that matter. I'm not such a fan of coffee."

Tony's briskness faded, and Nate saw a hand, covered in a bright-red wool mitten, reach out and pluck off Blaine's hat so the other hand could ruffle his curly hair. Tony stepped into Nate's vision and placed the hat carefully on Blaine's head before kissing him on the forehead.

"I know you're not," he said fondly. "I'm just as happy you prefer 'hot chocolate.'"

Blaine choked on a guffaw. "That was awful. Oh my God, I should break it off with you just for that!"

"You wouldn't really—" beat "—would you?"

"No. Oh *God*, no. I just need a minute, Tony. Just, let me swallow it all. Coming out, *moving out*, is . . . irrevocable. I want to be sure."

"The fact that you take it so seriously? That's why I love you. That's why it's worth the wait. Just know that all I want for both of us is— Is there a Yiddish word for 'everything'?"

"I don't know," Blaine said softly, and they were standing so close!

"That's what I want for you," Tony said, and this time the kiss was personal, intimate, on the lips.

Nate couldn't look away.

Alz. Alz is the word. That's what you want for each other. Alz. Isn't that what we wanted, Walter? Isn't that what you wanted for us? Wasn't that what we were looking for, listening for, with the bells?

But Walter didn't answer, and Nate watched in frustration as Blaine's Tony disappeared into the night, looking for the coffee shop. The lights around them, from the streets, from the cars, were swallowed up, and the darkness washed over his vision like a closed shutter, and when the shutter opened again, he was back, back in 1943, before Walter, before Carmen, when his world was narrowed to the tiny bunk with Hector and Joey and the missions he flew and the danger and the horror of a war that had swallowed the world . . .

RECON

"That's a dame!" Joey Shanahan muttered after a low whistle. "Hey, Meyer. Did you get that shot?"

Nate glanced up from the viewfinder of his 35mm Leica Rangefinder and whistled, pretending he'd noticed the pretty WAAF officer walking across the field of Harrington.

He hadn't. He'd been framing the big, powerful B-4 bombers instead.

"Yeah, you should get a picture!" Joey nodded, decidedly enthusiastic. Joey had apparently been striking out with women on a regular basis. He wasn't a bad-looking kid, really, Nate thought objectively. He stood average height, with dark-blond hair and blue eyes—the picture of the Irish people in the same way Nate was the picture of Jewish descent—and his mouth was wide and smiled easily. He even had sort of a crooked-grinned charm, but oy! Could that boy talk!

"You know, you should take a lot more pictures of dames in your spare time, you know that? I mean, you get the air base, the crowds, the seashore—why don't you got any dames?"

"For one thing, I don't call them that," Nate said, pulling a corner of his mouth up in faint derision. He liked Joey, liked him fine. If he was taking pictures of people right now, he'd take a picture of Joey, eyes as guileless as the sea. But Joey seemed to be incredibly single-minded about the thing—the one thing—Nate had never had a particular interest in. Oh yes, Nate did admire a pretty girl sometimes; pretty girls made pretty pictures. But he wasn't interested in spending his leave in some strange woman's bed. It wasn't kosher—there was supposedly *no* joy in that sort of sex, and while Nate's parents hadn't been Orthodox, they had raised him in the traditions out of a sense of obligation if nothing else.

And, well… girls just didn't appeal. Not even a little, not to touch, not to linger over. But the new mission—*that's* what appealed to him.

The missions were risky, which held an allure all its own. Risk meant you were doing your part, right? And flying in low in the middle of the night, dropping the M46 photoflash bombs to take pictures—it didn't get much riskier than that. So much for his father saying Nate wasn't a real man with the camera, that he couldn't do his part with a degree in art history and no military skills whatsoever. Nate had been in the cockpit for six Joker missions thus far, and every damned one of them scared the hell out of him.

Of course, Joey and Hector were flying Red Stockings, and those weren't a joke, either. They had to fly at high altitude, find a specific spot, and circle until Hector picked up the signal from the OSS officer who'd been dropped behind enemy lines earlier. Tough gig for Joey, circling around and around like that while Hector fiddled with the recording equipment to find the signal. Tougher still for the guy on the ground transmitting information and requesting information back—and hoping not to get killed!

Nate's pilot, Captain Albert Thompson, RAF, was a stolid sort—late thirties, lived for his weekly letter from his wife and two children. Nate depended on him to get them home safely, and Albert depended on Nate to competently assure him that their foray into darkness hadn't been in vain. Together, they were nothing like the fiery Hector and Joey, and Nate appreciated that. Three nights before, they'd been over Belgium when they'd been spotted by the Jerries. Albert had flown, closed mouthed, until they'd reached the air territory over St. Croix, and the stationed Allied planes had moved in and intercepted while Nate had taken pictures with a quiet resolve. Of course, it was dark, and even with his training and the special lens, Nate had only a general notion as to what he was looking for. But that didn't matter, now did it? What mattered was that his pictures would be developed and analyzed, and the installations he was photographing would either be announced useful for the war effort or too crowded with civilians to destroy. Either way, it was necessary information to have, and Nate was proud.

"What's wrong with calling a girl a dame? Hector, did you hear that? He thinks I'm not a gentleman enough to get a girl!" Joey sat at a folding card table in the sun outside their barracks, doing nav calculations for their next run. Most guys did their calculations once, twice, and then they were through, but Joey didn't make it through high school before he started working at his father's bar. He was smart, whip smart, and he wasn't going to let anybody say that some uneducated Mick blew a mission because he couldn't do the goddamned math.

"You're not," Hector said, grinning. He leaned up against the door with his face to the thin English sun. Having spent his whole life in Southern California, he was only truly happy when his bronze skin was glutted with sunshine, like an exotic houseplant or a napping cat. So far, England had proved a vast disappointment to him, but Hector wasn't the complaining sort. Nobody at this base even knew what Chanukah was, which was why Nate had given Hector a postcard of St. Croix for *Christmas* so he'd always have a little sunshine. Hector hadn't said much at the time, but he slept on one of the bottom bunks, and the postcard was right above him every time he woke.

"I am too a gentleman," Joey muttered, mapping out his nav coordinates for the third time. "If I wasn't a gentleman, I wouldn't do such a good job of escorting you home!"

Hector laughed loudly, with his mouth open, as though he expected everyone to share the joy. Nate loved that about him: he was unapologetic about who he was. He spoke Spanish with a big, booming voice and proudly displayed a picture of himself, dancing with his girl, in a zoot suit that he claimed to be sky blue and gold, and spoke of fondly. "Me and the other pachucos, we'd dance the sailor boys to shame, you know?" Even after the riots, Hector showed that photo, because he wasn't going to run scared just because the sailor boys had no sense of humor.

"Yeah, you take real good care of me, sweetheart. But maybe try those skills on someone who hasn't seen you scratch your balls and your ass and brag about it while in the shower."

Nate laughed, and after a year in the service, he didn't even blush. He'd gone to a private school, and while boys could get crude in the locker rooms anywhere, it was when they said things like that out under the sun, where even women could hear you, that had made Nate uncomfortable at first. But only at first.

But then, he'd been watching Joey Shanahan scratch his balls and his ass simultaneously for nearly three months—ever since he'd been assigned here, specialized camera equipment and all. There weren't so many OSS officers here at Menwith Hill that Nate could afford to alienate his roommate because he didn't like the way the guy talked about scratching his balls.

Besides, watching Joey check and recheck the calculations reminded Nate of what Hector had said repeatedly: Joey wasn't letting anyone die on his watch, particularly not the guy who had his back whenever they went looking for girls.

"You like it," Joey retorted. "If you didn't see me scratch my ass in the morning, you'd forget you needed that extra blanket to keep your pansy ass warm."

Hector squinted at the gray sky and shuddered. "Nobody's warm today, that's for certain."

No, not on this chilly day in March.

"It would be this cold in New York," Nate said, thinking. He found he didn't miss his family's brownstone or his father's small watch shop at all. He hadn't waited for Pearl Harbor, no. Nate had watched, along with the rest of his family, as the Nazis had become more than just a frightening rumor, threatening their kin overseas, and metamorphosed into a terrifying, mind-twisting reality. Friends' cousins had disappeared, letters had ceased, pleas to the State Department for news had gone unheeded. Nate's Uncle Lev, whom he had never met, became a ghost on the tongues of his father and mother, overnight, one more mortal caution to haunt the brownstone, next to Nate's dead brother and the children his mother's body had not been able to sustain.

"Yeah?" Hector asked. He pulled a cigarette from the ever-present pack in his pocket and offered one to Joey. Joey demurred, because he was still working and he didn't smoke when he was working, and Nate simply didn't smoke. At first the guys had assumed it was because he was a Jew; that he was too fastidious to like the taste was beyond them.

"Yes," Nate said, staring at the grayness ruminatively. "In fact, it would be even more bitter." He cracked a smile. "Of course, in New York, they don't have to put on flight gear and go miles into the air."

A sudden silence descended then. There was a big push tonight in the 654th. More than two hundred of the men stationed at Menwith Hill were with tactical surveillance, and Nate figured that between him and Hector, they'd counted over twenty planes that were going up this night. Not a weather advance, which meant more dogfights and more casualties, but a surveillance push. Several planes going off to all quarters of Europe, some Joker, some Red Stocking, all of them with urgent orders that they didn't share with anyone else. American, RAF—everybody was going up in the sky to see what was what.

Nate, who only played chess a little, thought about the way the old men in the park would sit back, surveying the entire board over their noses before letting go of a long, considering breath.

This moment right here was the Allied equivalent of sitting back, sliding their hands under their suspenders, and saying, *Hmm, what is it we have to work with here*, before beginning the game in earnest.

Sometimes, an awful lot of pawns would be left, rolling alongside the board, before those moments behind the chessboard ended. Nate worried about those pawns like he worried about the entire board. In fact, he worried more.

"Hey," Hector said lowly, in the kind of voice that made Nate sidle a little closer, even aware that he and Joey were the only ones within earshot anyway.

"Yeah?"

"Where're you going tonight?" Hector asked. "I mean, not specific-like, just, you know. Country at least, okay?"

"Germany," Nate said without compunction for spilling secrets. There *were* no secrets between the three of them. "But I don't know specifically where. You?"

"France. Some place called Provence Claire La Lune. Our operators down there say we might talk to some resistance fighters— our guys are supposed to encourage that, you know what I mean?"

"Yeah? Well, that's a good thing."

"I know it. What about you?"

Nate grunted. "The usual—take a picture at these coordinates— again? Got no clue. A month later, those coordinates are pulverized to powder. Or not."

Hector grunted back. "It's not personal enough," he growled. "The Jerries, they don't like the color of our skin, who our parents are—feels like a knee to the balls. We go five miles up and listen to voices—"

"Or two miles up and take pictures of clouds," Nate finished for him. "Yes. Impersonal means for a very personal war. I understand. But what's to do? Our skills weren't marching and shooting, they were pictures and listening. It's what we can—"

"You ready?" Albert stalked around the corner in midconversation. Well, he often did that—he didn't like small talk for one thing. For another, he was in charge of settling new recruits. He met with his staff sergeants in the morning—the mother hen of the Menwith Hill barracks. He was busy, and he had no time to worry about OSS recruits with one lousy skill.

"We're not going until . . ." Nate left the end meaningfully. He hadn't been given a time; that was Albert's purview.

"Twenty-one hundred," Albert told him shortly. "Be outfitted and ready to belt in, yeah?" As though Nate had ever *not* been ready to belt in. "Meet me on the field, no fucking off to spank your monkey or bugger the rabbi or whatever the hell else you blokes do."

"Yes, sir!" Nate saluted, because Albert was a superior officer and for no other reason. "Sir?" he asked, when it looked like Albert was going to stomp off.

"Yes, Lieutenant?"

"Where we going tonight?"

Albert grimaced. Yes, all destinations were classified, but it did help a photographer to know what he was dealing with. Albert called Nate over with a jerk of the head, and Nate left off his insouciant pose against the barracks.

"Stuttgart, like that means anything to you," he said, voice low enough for Joey and Hector to be left out. "Looks like there'll be good cloud cover, but there's nothing friendly for pretty much everywhere. Be prepared to keep a sharp lookout and not just through the viewfinder. Can you do that or is it some sort of holy day?"

"I'm up for the job, sir!" Nate saluted again, and Albert glared, then stalked off. A good pilot, but not a kind man, at least not to Nate. And it was clear his heart was so very with the family he saw once a month on leave. Well, good for him. He could see family on leave.

Nate couldn't—and apparently Hector and Joey could only get *hints* of getting laid, and not all of that was Joey's fault.

"Really, Meyer," Joey asked, looking up from his calculations and leaning on his elbows, "what did you do to that guy?"

"Besides make him fly reconnaissance?" Nate asked with a shrug. "I have no idea. You think it's because I'm a Jew?" That was rhetorical, of course.

"They don't got Jews in England? Get out!" Hector laughed, turning his head to spit. "I thought that was Hitler's problem. They got Jews everywhere!"

Nate raised an eyebrow. "We're not cockroaches, but yes. Jews populate Europe much like Catholics—wherever there is a warm place to breed."

Hector and Joey didn't take offense; they laughed instead. No, you could not spend months smelling your roommates' farts and not learn to be tolerant of one another's differences. Of course, Hector had started to thaw with the postcard of St. Croix. With Joey, it had taken a tiny gold pin of the cross, which Joey wore on his hat, underneath the brim. Not Nate's faith, no, but then, giving it some honor had made Joey feel like it wasn't under attack by Nate's very "otherness." He had friends from college who would have been angry at this—why should Nate pacify the ignorant?

But Hector had his zoot suits, and Joey had his crosses, and Nate had the six-pointed star he wore under his shirt with his dog tags on every mission. His father may have thought Nate was weak for becoming friends with the gentiles, but Nate had to believe that faith and goodness were things to respect. Wasn't that what his own faith taught?

He had only needed to spend a week playing cards, listening to Joey's record player, and exchanging family stories with Hector, to know that if these men didn't come back from their mission, or the next, or the next, he should be very sorry.

"Have we all put our letters under our pillows?" Nate asked carefully in the silence following Albert's departure.

"Same letter as last time." Joey grunted. "I'm starting to think it's a good luck charm."

"Yeah, well, as much as the captain hates me, I'm thinking I can take all the luck I can get."

Hector grunted in return. "I'd let Joey here fly you, but he's the only one who doesn't scare the hell out of me at thirty thousand." Hector shuddered. "*Dios.* What a man like me is doing in that much cold, I don't even want to think about."

Nate smiled at him, liking him very much. "Penance," he said, eyes twinkling. "For all the bad deeds you've left to do."

Hector laughed again, and Nate felt an unfortunate stir in the pit of his stomach. *No. No. Not this.* Not this, that had kept him aloof from his fellows through school. Not this, fear of seeing the sun on a cheekbone, filtered through someone's eyelashes, or the shadow of a jawline, and feeling . . . this thing. The thing that poets spoke about, but not like this. Not for the girls at the dances with their shy smiles and sturdy prettiness but for the boys, milling about on the other side of the room in navy shirts and red ties, looking, by turns, bored and nervous and happy.

"I haven't done anything *truly* bad yet," Hector said, chuckling low and evil. Then he kicked Joey's chair. "I've got an albatross around my neck keeping me from all the wickedness!"

Joey cast him an irritated glance. "Yeah, and it's called a dame in the States. Now gimme two more seconds, and we can go do some PT before we go up!"

"I'll go change," Nate said, because his camera equipment was flawless, as it always was, and because whoever thought of doing PT before a mission had been inspired. Getting the blood flowing and the muscles pleasantly exercised took away some of the feeling of confinement in the small space of the cockpit, and some of the restlessness, as well. Not too much—not enough to tire one out—just enough to make the body easier at rest.

And it was a perfect excuse to get away from Hector and his bronzed skin and square face and the way his brown eyes seemed to invite everyone in on the joke.

Nate was buttoning up his loose khakis and lacing his softest boots when he decided to check under the pillow for his letter. Ah, yes, there it was. A good-bye to his mother, and a passing nod to his father.

His throat tightened.

Was that all he wanted to offer? His father was a reserved man, certainly—open affection had never been his way. But was Nate's enmity an adult feeling or the leftovers of childhood resentment? Nate frowned at the envelope, made of some of the best paper stock Joey had been able to smuggle out of the officers' supply cabinet, and wondered if he shouldn't write another letter. Something more genial, more neutral. Something, perhaps, asking his father to believe he was worthwhile, that he was capable of worthwhile things. Something apologizing for not being Zev.

Nate's conscience was perfectly clear about the things he'd done in the war thus far. The tally of things that bothered him or made him question his faith at this moment equaled the number of times his father had ever kissed his cheek in affection: zero.

He heard a ruckus behind him as Hector and Joey entered, pushing on each other and laughing. No time to rewrite the letter now. He shoved it back under the pillow and ran after his roommates for a round of pop-up in the field by the airstrip. None of the other pilots or officers joined them—they never had. Many of the residents were RAF, for one, and the rivalry was not always easy to transcend. For many, the mix was too different. The spic, the Mick, and the Jew—it was the beginning of a joke with no good punch line. Nate, who had never had a peer group through school, had finally managed to find one, and they were as isolated unto themselves as three as Nate ever had been as one.

But at least they were three.

Maybe next leave, Nate would go with them and let Hector try to find him a woman. Maybe those moments of thinking Hector Garcia was as beautiful as sunlight would fade.

Nate had a notion that being inside a real mosquito was probably much quieter than being inside of a de Havilland DH.98 Mosquito—wooden sides or not. The airplanes were versatile— light bombers, tactical bombers, day or night missions, and, of course, converted photo-surveillance planes. While the top sported the squadron insignia, as well as Captain Thompson's personal insignia—a mosquito wearing a flowered dress with a purse—near the cockpit, the bottom of Miss Mossy (as the captain called her) had been painted dark gray to blend in with the nighttime cloud cover. Still, Nate had always been surprised that every plane that went flying over German airspace hadn't been shot down.

"Stuttgart," Nate said resignedly into the intercom as the plane took off. "Five shots at the coordinates. We have ten flares."

"I know the mission," Captain Thompson stated flatly. "I know the mission, I know the risks. Do you need me to hold your hand?"

"Only if it would help you feel better," Nate replied just as flatly.

Thompson grunted, the sound translating over the intercom as a crackle of static. "Not bloody likely. Do you have anything else obvious you'd like to tell me? Do I take a right or a left to get to Germany? How's that? Can you tell me how to fly this boat to Germany, you uppity shit?"

"I assume you point it east and go," Nate snapped. "Wake me up when we get there."

But Nate had no intention of sleeping.

The view through the cockpit window wasn't ideal. Nate had thought more than once that he wished he could fly facedown on a clear platform so that he could see everything—the countryside, the farms, the smokestacks, everything. Because even with the hum of the Mosquito in his ears, when he gazed down on the sleeping mass of Europe, he knew he wasn't seeing the complete vista, and the artist that he was hungered for the whole picture.

Bombs would be dropped on some of the towns down there; devastation would follow. What would that look like? Who would be killed? He was skilled with the specialized camera and the twenty-four-inch lens that allowed him to take shots from the plane, although the pictures he usually shot needed a room full of intelligence officers with magnifying glasses to pinpoint exactly what the photo targets were. What he was not skilled at was understanding the distance between the plane, at fifteen thousand feet, and the people on the ground. Empty space? The handbreadth of God? What made it so someone such as he could determine whether people he would never see or touch would live or die?

The silence in the plane became oppressive, and Nate scanned through his viewfinder to keep himself from sleeping in earnest. The shiny, roiling mass of the ocean sat underneath them, but the horizon of France and Germany was not that far away. *Oh, hey*—a town, smaller than Stuttgart, right across the black silver of the channel.

"Hello, what's that?" Nate murmured to himself. "Do you see that?"

"I don't see it!" Captain Thompson snapped back, but Nate was too preoccupied with what looked to be large smokestacks coming from the ground, just north of the tiny city below, to respond to his tone. That couldn't be right, could it? There would have to be an installation underground. He couldn't see in the dark—or without his camera.

"Captain, give us a candle drop—"

"Those are saved for the—"

"I know, but we've got ten. We'll only need two. I just want one."

"I don't like it—we're hours away from Stuttgart."

"Do you see anyone, Captain? There's no one out tonight, and that . . . that thing down there. It looks like a plant. It wasn't there the last time we flew up this way, and it just feels wrong—it's something important, can't you feel it?"

"Could give a shit what you feel, you fuckin'—"

"Captain, do you really want to finish that sentence?" Nate asked, his skin chilling underneath his voluminous flight suit.

"Yes, damn it!" Thompson snapped, but he didn't. "Candle dropping. Where do you want to go?"

"That town below us—it's small. You see the outskirts of it to the east a little. Yes. There. Go."

"Count off," Thompson snarled, and Nate held his breath. There. They were close. Close. Close.

"Launch candle in ten-nine-eight-seven-six-five-four-three-two— Candle launch!"

Thompson hit something on the dash, and the flare cascaded out of the plane, falling, falling, falling before exploding harsh and white, lighting up the sky around them.

Nate was ready.

He clicked the shutter furiously, all of the settings ready for nighttime pictures. One, two, three, four—the light began to stutter—five, six.

"*Shit*!" Thompson cried, and Nate finished his last shot and looked around. *Oh hell.* Sure enough, framed against the clouds by the stuttering flare was a pair of Messerschmitts.

"Can you—"

"Shut up and let me call for backup," Thompson barked, and Nate heard him radio for a couple of bulldogs to come take care of the Messers on their tail.

And then Captain Thompson did what was best for everyone involved and flew that little plane as fast as it could go.

The Messerschmitts weren't going anywhere. They stayed on their tail, firing occasionally but lacking the necessary range. Miss Mossy had a lead on them from the very beginning, and if Captain Albert knew one thing, it was how to fly quick like zoom.

"Where's the bloody bulldogs?" Captain Thompson snarled. "What's the good of having planes out with guns if they can't shoot that bloody lot out of the fucking sky?"

Nate wisely didn't answer. He changed the film in his camera in tense silence, putting the canister in the cargo pocket of his flight suit and readying the camera for Stuttgart on faith.

They didn't make it.

The Messerschmitt Bf 110 was a superlative night fighter, and Miss Mossy, who was fitted out with cameras all around, had no guns. Her cooling system had been modified to keep the cameras *and* the pilots from freezing during the high-altitude missions, and when pushed too hard, her engines tended to get hot. Even while Nate despised Captain Albert, he knew the man was flying a fine line between outrunning the enemy and cooking their engines with speed.

Their one hope was that the call for backup would be answered and some dogfighters would appear over the horizon around them.

Nate kept lookout, and when the first bursts of fire spurted from the newly appeared specks behind them, acute relief almost stopped his voice.

"Friendlies!"

"Brilliant. We might not die up here."

"I am not overwhelmed with optimism," Nate muttered, but either Thompson's voice was lost in the engine noise or he didn't deign to answer.

Below, the various lumps and smokestacks of Stuttgart appeared. Very few lights—all sides had learned the trick of the blackout to confuse bombing raids—but Nate had flown over and taken pictures before. He knew the shape, the basic landmarks—and although he knew their support was behind them and if they couldn't outrun the Messerschmitts before the bulldogs got there they were in real trouble, for some reason the city gave him comfort. It wasn't featureless, wasn't blank. He recognized the landscape, and they weren't lost.

And just as he figured it out, tracers of antiaircraft fire passed to his right, shattering his peace.

"They're closing in!"

"Not them! It's another group! Hang on and spot the bastards!"

Calmly, Nate placed his camera and lens in the case and buckled it shut, using his stomach muscles and thighs to keep his seat as the plane began a series of vicious evasive maneuvers that might have made his stomach rebel when he'd first started to fly. When the camera was safely stowed, he grabbed hold of the grips on either side and did what Captain Thompson had ordered: held on and spotted.

"Three o'clock, Cap. Two planes closing."

"Dive roll. Don't puke."

"They're following, following—lost them. Not puking."

"Don't be a bloody arse! Fire from six o'clock. G roll."

Oh hell. The negative-G rolls—Captain Thompson's specialty—were Nate's least favorite aerobatic. He held on and didn't puke—his first time up in the cockpit, he *had* puked, and had to live in it for hours. Never again.

"Nine o'clock, Cap—friendlies."

"Fucking firing! Blast it and bugger God's arse!"

The blasphemy didn't faze Nate, but the fact that they were stuck between friendly fire and enemy fire without guns themselves was starting to wear on his hard-earned calm.

"Evade, Captain. Friendlies engaging!"

"I am evading, you stupid kike. Shut the fuck up and let me work!"

Oy! Now they get to the bottom of Captain Albert's hostility? "For heaven's sake," Nate muttered, but Thompson let out another round of cursing, and the plane jerked, shuddered, and rolled some more. They had flown past Stuttgart now, beyond the borders, and dropped their altitude in an attempt to evade. The featureless landscape loomed below them, a black trough of rural woods.

"Holy God, there's more!"

"You had to stop and take a fucking picture!" Thompson snarled. "We had one lousy job to do, and you had to stop and take a fucking picture, and we've got these buggers following us from fucking *everywhere!*"

"Well, that means whatever was there was pretty damned important, don't you think?" Nate shot back, because that was the truly frightening thing. Stuttgart was a big city, pretty close to the border of France and Germany; there *should* be important things in Stuttgart. But that smaller city, on the tip of land across from England, the Axis shouldn't be making anything there, should they?

"We're not bloody likely to find out, are we?"

They executed a barrel roll evasive maneuver then, the horizon spinning dizzily and leaving Nate gasping for breath in the hopes that he wouldn't throw up and wouldn't pass out. Captain Thompson swore again, and the plane suddenly lurched in the middle of a barrel roll.

"We're hit!" Thompson screamed. "We're hit! And I'm going to die because a bloody kike Jew had to jerk off his camera!"

Later, it would occur to Nate that for all his shortcomings as a companion, Albert Thompson was an amazing pilot. The plane heaved level, which saved his life, and descended at a terrifying, dizzying speed. Too fast to jettison, even if bailing out of a Mosquito was possible at this altitude, but slow enough to keep the plane from disintegrating on impact. Maybe.

The wood under his feet trembled, and the plane skittered and rattled, shaking Nate like a yolk in its shell. Something exploded behind him, the force of air blowing Nate forward, then back, until he cracked his head on the window and the world detonated into the blackness inside his skull.

WALTER

Pain—aching, slicing, ripping pain—in his side, in his arm and shoulder, in his thigh.

And heat, humid, like the residual warmth of a hot summer day, seeping through his many layers of flight suit, leaving him nauseated, disoriented, weeping with discomfort.

"Shut up. I'm getting there."

The voice was so unexpected, the flat accent of the American Midwest like a slap in the face.

"I'm sorry, I'm sorry," Nate mumbled, his eyes at half-mast. "I'm sorry, I didn't know . . ."

Didn't know what? What didn't Nate know? Had he forgotten to mention something as the plane had landed?

"I didn't know, either," the voice said, sounding disgruntled and irritated. "One minute I was sleeping, and the next minute, I got a plane screaming down on me. Caught completely by surprise."

Sounds—unfamiliar sounds. Tree-snapping, tortured-foliage sounds, and that flat Midwestern snap, swearing at it all.

"You swear like a thug," Nate muttered, his breath coming short. *Your ribs, you think? Yes. Yes, and they've punctured a lung.* "Do you know what it is? To doctor a rib?" Nate asked, out loud apparently.

"Yeah, I can do that," the voice said. "You're sounding sort of breathy. Probably a punctured lung. I can do that too."

"So it was a lucky thing I crashed here then," Nate said, hearing his mother in his head. *Oh, so your father is the worst thing to happen to you? Well, it's a lucky thing you were born into this family or you would have nothing to complain about, would you?*

His unseen companion laughed a bitter cackle, crackling like twigs, dry and ready to light. "Not so lucky for your pilot," he said, voice almost gentle.

"Isn't that nice. You're worried I have lost a friend." That *was* nice. It was something Hector or even Joey might do.

"Haven't you?"

Nate grimaced. He did not like to speak ill of the dead but... "He cursed me for a filthy kike with his last breath," Nate said, feeling tired. It wasn't until he said it that he realized a man with this voice might just stalk off and leave Nate to die in this cockpit in the middle of... *Gott*, where?

"Well, that was damned foolish of him," the voice said practically. "But he did do you the favor of deploying the canopy—that was good of him."

"He was probably planning to eject," Nate muttered. "Not that he'd tell me."

"Humph. Those of us who aren't Jewish would call that an asshole. What would *you* call it?"

Nate grunted. His eyes were closed but the silver specks behind his closed lids swam and scattered like amphibious birds. "*Schtik dreck*," he said succinctly, his father's Yiddish coming to him unbidden when he'd tried so hard to leave it behind him. "Filthy, worthless piece of—"

"I get it!" the voice said gleefully. "You're damned feisty for a Jew. I thought you people were all about peace and acceptance."

"You've never met my father," Nate mumbled.

There had been clattering and clambering, the sound of feet on the wooden paneling off the wing, the hollow thudding and rustling of tree limbs, the thump of someone walking on something not designed to be used as a doormat.

Rough hands, brusque and practical, worked the latches on Nate's belts and those around his shoulders.

"You got anything in this wreck we can use for food or tinder?" asked the voice attached to the hands.

"Under the seats, I think," Nate told him. "GI rations. Can burn the plane for tinder."

"The coating on it might make it burn black, but if we're still here come winter, I'll think about it."

The voice was so practical. Nate forced himself to open his eyes to put a face to it.

Small. Narrow chin, narrow cheekbones, middling brow. Eyes that were probably blue-green in the sun, with lashes that started out orange and turned white at the tips, even in the moonlight. The healthy scattering of freckles across what was still a fair-skinned face, and a military cap with the brim turned up.

A lean, pursed mouth, minimized with concentration.

Nate's brain framed the shot, clicked the shutter; the picture would be there in his mind forever.

The man wasn't looking at Nate's face—he was too busy assessing Nate's body through the flight suit—but Nate was struck with the urge to brush his fingertip along one of the nearly transparent eyebrows.

So pale. Translucent. Like an angel.

A pain center detonated inside Nate's body, and all thoughts of angels were forgotten. His brain was murky with images of blood clouds in black ink, and he let out a cry.

"Yeah, sorry 'bout that," the young man muttered. "'Kay, gonna pull you outta there. Gonna fuckin' hurt. Your plane's the only one that went down, so feel free to make all the noise you want."

"Reassuring," Nate panted, but when his rescuer clambered into the tiny space in front of the pilot's seat, reached down into Nate's cockpit, and hauled him up by the armpits, he let out a bellow that probably startled birds.

Swinging his leg up, over, and around the edge of the plane was one of the bravest things Nate had ever done. The pressure in his stomach, against his ribs, defied description.

He couldn't remember sliding down the wing after that, although he must have. The man next to him was short—barely five foot six, and Nate was a big, strapping man. Nate had to have borne some of his own weight, right?

He certainly was moving his own legs when he came to his senses minutes later, although he was leaning heavily on his new companion.

"Captain Thompson," he gasped, although he had hardly any wind at all to do so. "Must get . . ."

"Dead, remember?" The smaller man was panting too, holding up most of Nate's greater weight. "And besides, he sounds like an asshole. Not sure I want to go out of my way to save an asshole."

Nate stumbled, and his side and thigh and arm twisted, his vision grayed around the edges, and he couldn't draw the breath to defend his captain. *Why defend him? The soldier is right.*

Was that what he was? A soldier? He had a uniform cap on, wool, with corporal's bars on it. So, not a private—not an officer, either.

"Where . . ." Oh God, his voice was barely a whisper. "Where are we going?"

"Do you even know where you are?"

Cocky man. "Moselle?"

"God, you're good! I ain't had any idea where I am. I'm talking *months*. So, yeah. Moss-ell. Some fuckin' woods not far from Germany. That's where we are, and that's where we're going. You're all caught up now."

If he'd had the energy, Nate would have either laughed or glared. He wasn't sure which. "A military station? A home? A hole—" *Ah! Hells, that hurts!* He couldn't see where to put his feet in the darkness. "A magical hospital in the woods?"

"A cottage out of *Snow White*, no dwarves?"

They burst into a clearing then, and Nate sucked in a gasp of air that almost killed him. "I thought . . . you were . . ."

"Joking. Lucky you, everything's here but the broad with the broom. C'mon, airman. Let's take the stairs one at a time."

The front door was splintered at the catch, and the corporal simply nudged it with his shoulder, walking Nate inside to what appeared to be a rather neglected but once-charming house. The floor was sanded wood and the furniture sturdy, a low couch and love seat covered in faded-green brocade. The carpet had once been rich wool, but it had seen better days, and Nate had a sad impression of a house gutted by its inhabitants. Pictures had been swept off the mantel, large, bright squares and ovals stood out on the red velveteen wallpaper, and a desk in the corner stood with all of the drawers open. Rodents had apparently made a nest because jagged little bits were falling out of the drawer on the bottom. To their left, as they walked in, was an adjoining kitchen, not separated from the living room by so much as a partition.

"Broad, dame, skirt—why don't men just call them women?" Nate wondered out loud. "They're much less frightening when you call them women."

"What does calling them women get you that calling them anything else don't?" Corporal Manners wanted to know.

"I'm told it gets you dates," Nate said drunkenly. "I wouldn't know myself— *Gah*!"

Corporal Manners sat him in the middle of the couch and swung his legs around to the end. He struggled with Nate's flight jacket, unbuttoning the cuffs and sliding the gloves off first, leaving it open like a butterfly under Nate's back and Nate in his blood-soaked undershirt.

Boots next—the soft ones—black socks, and flight pants—wool—peeled painfully off, the fabric sticking to the wounds at Nate's hips and thighs. All painful, bleeding, in need of bandaging if not stitching, but nothing so bad as the ribs and the aching, wet feeling in the left side of his chest.

"This is lovely," Nate murmured, feeling relief from the heat, from the pressure. Oh yeah, sure, his body still hurt, but it was getting floaty and faraway. "If you're going to drift in the clouds, this isn't a bad place to drift fr— *Augh*!"

His companion was back. Where had he gone? Wherever it was, he'd returned with what looked like a shaving kit, a sewing kit, and a toolbox, and he'd pulled it all from the same black bag.

And he'd just poked what seemed to be a rubber tube in through a hole in Nate's chest. Slow, slow, past flesh, bouncing off the bone of his rib, skating to the side, following the path of the wound . . .

Nate's throat was raw from screaming, and the sharp smell of alcohol and carbolic burned the tissues of his nose with every inhale.

He felt a pop, and a cold, peculiar, wrenching sensation followed. With his next breath, he felt as though a hot, wet press of wool had been lifted from his chest.

He breathed in again and heard a faint whistling, felt some weakness throughout his body, then a movement at his side and his companion was doing something odd to the tube.

"This is a valve," the guy said. "What you're going to do is, whenever you feel like you're not getting enough air, open it like this, see?"

Nate nodded. Yes, of course he saw. It was disturbing, to see that thing sticking out of his side. But he was falling asleep, pain graying the world, everything—abandoned house, quirky little rescuer—fading at the edges.

"I cannot do that while I'm sleeping," Nate said, for clarity's sake.

"Yeah, I hear you. Catch some winks. I'll be here."

It should not have been reassuring. Nate closed his eyes, and he saw that terrible, helter-skelter jumble of treetops in the dark, the tracer of AAF, the darkened sky, the darker earth, and he heard Captain Thompson's voice in his ear, shouting obscenities because he didn't want to die with a Jew.

He opened his eyes again and saw his new companion. The man was leaning against the chair by the couch, legs sprawled, eyes closed in apparent sleep as the dawn crept through the cracks in the boarded-up windows.

"I can feel you looking at me," the boy said laconically. "Is this a test to see if I'll wake up?"

"No," Nate said, exhausted, and relieved somewhat, because now he trusted that the boy *would* wake. "I was just wondering about you."

"Wondering what?" He opened one eye. "'Cause you need your rest and no one wants to hear my life story."

Nate did—later. "I would settle for your name," he said on a yawn.

The young man smiled lazily. "Walter. Corporal Walter Phillips of the 185th."

Nate closed his eyes, thought hard. "The 185th? Aren't you supposed to be in Africa?"

Walter laughed shortly. "Yeah. Ain't life a motherfucker? And you are . . .?" The chill of dawn crept in, and Nate was reminded that it was March and the heat must have been imagined. Walter was dressed in a plain men's long-sleeved shirt, too large for him, and wool pants, the same.

He was thinking dreamily that his companion would look charming in clothes that fit when the question seeped in.

"Nathan Selig Meyer. Call me Nate."

"'Kay, Nate. Get some shut-eye. I ain't heard another person breathing in this house since there was snow up to my waist outside. Believe me, I'll notice when you stop."

"You are such a comfort," Nate muttered.

"And you're a sarcastic bastard. I like that in a man whose life I just saved. Now go to sleep."

Nate, who'd called Captain Thompson "Captain Albert" just to irritate him, actually took an order from a corporal and closed his eyes.

The next several hours were confusion. Walter flipped his valve several times to let air into his lung, and the pain there, in his side, was tremendous. Strips of ripped linen were wrapped around his ribs. Even more had been made into gauze pads and tied to his leg and his hip.

Before that, though, there was the washing, and Nate did not acquit himself well during that. No, he didn't thrash around and abuse the poor man trying to clean his wounds, but he did cry and moan and use several swear words that he hadn't been aware he knew.

After all of that, he found himself apologizing.

"I am sorry for all that racket," he said humbly. "I don't mean to be a bad patient after all you have done."

"You're not a bad patient," Walter replied smartly. "You're a *loud* patient, but you're never mean. And I appreciate that you grab the couch instead of belting me one. Man, I'd be black and blue after the medic tent."

"You're a medic?" Seemed a stupid, obvious question, but Nate would learn that nothing was ever obvious with Walter.

"Nope, not at first," Walter said. He had a basin of water and carbolic next to the bed and washed his hands in it as he spoke. The basin was already red, but Nate had seen him go to the pump at the kitchen sink and wash again and again, so Nate wasn't worried. "When we landed in Tunisia, most of our platoon got wiped out as we were coming ashore. Just me and Jimmy were left, and Jimmy was hurting. Took him to the medic tent and . . ."

When Walter looked away, his face was so twisted in misery that Nate couldn't remember his own pain.

"I am so sorry. You miss your friend?"

"We were—" Walter shook his head. "Ain't no good words for us. And he died, and I had nothin'—no captain, no squad, no platoon.

But I was in the medic tent and used to bein' useful. I don't know how long we were there—a month? Two? Landed in November, followed the army to Morocco, but the medic tent kept me. Guess I really was useful. Learned all sorts of stuff." Walter stood and grabbed the basin, walking to the sink with it. There was a wood-burning stove in the kitchen, and he had a pot set there to boil most times, Nate noticed. Now, he put his instruments in it—scissors, a scalpel, the needle he'd used to repair the gash in Nate's thigh and hip—and left them to boil while he rinsed out the bowl and washed his hands.

Nate watched him do these things from the corner of his eye and was reassured. It was not easy to keep clean, or to keep the instruments clean, but Walter made a good effort.

"You seem to have learned a lot," Nate sallied, mindful that he still didn't have enough wind to speak very loudly. "They gave you your doctor's bag, right?"

"They did not," Walter said, shaking his hands rapidly to get rid of the excess moisture. "That came from somewhere else."

"Oh." It was a rebuff if Nate had ever heard one.

"Don't get your panties in a twist," Walter said, but not unkindly. "You're about done in, and that's not a good story." He dried his hands off on some of the same linen that he'd used to bind up Nate's wounds. It had faint blue stripes on it, and Nate recognized it as sheets—they had probably come with the house.

When his hands were dry, he stood near Nate and put his hand on his forehead. "Fuck. Fuck, you're warm. You're warm, and all that boiling bullshit didn't do any fucking good. Goddamn it—"

"Don't stop washing your hands," Nate begged. He had heard stories of the barbarian goyim doctors who did not value cleanliness like the Jewish ones. Watching Walter take all that care with sterilization had been reassuring.

"Wasn't planning on it. 'Bout the smartest thing the army ever taught me. But Jesus, are you hot. Fuck."

"Aspirin?" Nate asked. "Willow bark?"

"Is that some sort of a tree?" Walter looked at him sharply. "'Cause brother, they've got trees aplenty around here. You got no idea."

"Yes," Nate said, and he could feel it now, the surreal, achy, shivering cold that came with illness. His wounds were swollen, and the wide-gauge needle that let him breathe felt like a lead pipe shoved through his flesh. Walter said that eventually the lung would heal, and then they could extract the thing. Nate wondered if it was appropriate to dance on the day that happened.

Walter's hands patted his cheeks briskly. "Stay with me, Nate," he said, matter-of-fact. "You are *the* first human being I've talked to in nearly two months—I'd rather you not die. Now what in the hell does a willow tree look like?"

"We have them in the States," Nate said, remembering them in Central Park and planted in the spaces in the sidewalk. "They're beautiful trees, lots of hanging branches like cat tails, tiny leaves."

"Do they have furry things on them in the spring?" Walter asked excitedly. "'Cause nobody told me that's what that was. We got them—or this place has them. They're out behind the house. 'Kay, Nate, you stay with me here. I'll be back in a minute."

Walter's feet slapped the floorboards, flapping like a schoolboy's, as he ran out of the small elegant cottage, and for a moment, Nate was confused. *Zev? Zev, are you here? I thought you died—influenza, remember? You were the strongest of us. Father was so angry.*

That anxious *slap slap* returned, and a breath of sun-warmed air blew into the room.

"Is it really March? It feels much warmer than March," Nate murmured, feeling dreamy. It wasn't the same gray sky they had left in England, was it?

"It's the woods," Walter said frankly, and Nate smiled at him widely.

"Walter! I am so glad it is you. For a minute you sounded like Zevi, and he's been gone ten years. I was very confused."

"Yeah? Well, one minute you were talking about the weather and the next you were talking about your dead uncle. I should think so."

"Brother," Nate said without self-pity. "My older brother. Influenza. I got it too, but I lived."

"Mm." Walter grunted, clearly uncomfortable. "Well, I'm sorry to hear that. Let's see if you can live through this too. Here—is this the kind of tree you mean?"

He held up a few willow whips, the gray furry buds growing just large enough to sprout some green.

"Yes," Nate said, smiling through his shivers. "If you can strip the bark and boil it, it should take down the fever. My mother learned that from her *bubbe*, but she said that was for people in the old country." Nate laughed a little to himself before shivering some more. "Funny that she would remember that, though. Strange things our parents give us that we cannot give away or put on a shelf." He was sounding more and more like his grandmother and father just talking about them. Maybe it was being sick, but the New York Yiddish he'd worked so hard at suppressing was rising to the top, and he couldn't seem to stop it.

"Speak for yourself. My old man ain't given me nothin' I wanna keep." That flat, Midwestern voice was passionate and bitter. "Now hang tight for a bit, okay? Gonna take me some time to brew this up, and I don't want you going nowhere."

"I did have a formal dinner planned for eight o'clock," Nate said, laughing at himself. "I am going to have to give my regrets."

"You're a real card, you know that? You should go on the radio, that's what I think."

Nate chuckled. "Would they play big band music too? I would like to dance in a zoot suit, in purple like a king."

"I don't even know what in the hell that is." Walter's voice was fading in and out, and he was making free with the pots and pans in the kitchen. Nate grunted, and it turned into a whine. Always, always, the stove on, making the house so hot, and the smell of firewood permeated everything, almost worse than diesel oil and airplane fuel, which he could never get away from; it was even on the clothes he was wearing now.

"It's hot!" Nate shouted. "And my feet are sweating!"

"You are fucking delirious with fever is what you are!" Walter shouted back indignantly. "And you are the loudest son of a bitch I have *ever* heard. Now shut up, and gimme a chance to work!"

"Shut up? That man just told me to shut up. Heh heh heh. He should be my father!"

"I heard that! Now you're just being mean!"

Nate could never say why, but that struck him as being hilarious, humor of the highest order! That was Bergen and McCarthy right there! He was not sure how long he lay there, giggling, before Walter tapped him on the shoulder and, mindful of his wounds, helped him sit up.

"Mister, I do not know what you are like in your real regular life, but I have got to tell you that right now, you are a one-man vaudeville show."

Nate gasped in pain and thought it was hard to breathe. But he was thirsty, and not so out of his mind that he didn't know the bitter-smelling brew was his salvation. He grasped Walter's chapped, work-gnarled hands and steadied the cup to his lips. Sip, sip, sip. He took a breath and met Walter's bemused eyes over the brim of the thick ceramic mug.

"I am usually quite reserved," he said sincerely.

"That's a real shame," Walter said with equal honesty. "I could listen to you ramble all day."

He smiled then and winked, like it was all a big joke, but Nate saw something then, something haunted, something with the loneliness of a god.

"You are so sad. Such pretty eyes and so sad."

To his dismay, Walter looked even sadder. The lean mouth parted slightly, and the round, blue-green eyes grew shiny. "Now hurry up and finish it off," he urged. "'Cause when you get better, I know you ain't gonna remember that."

"It's hard to breathe," Nate said, and although he was not talking about the shunt in his lungs, that was what Walter did for him: fixed the valve so Nate could breathe. Nate took a more sober breath and finished off the bitter dregs of the willow bark tea. It would've been a lie to say he felt better—although the liquid down his throat had been nice—but he did feel cared for.

Walter laid him back down, grabbing a bolster from the high-backed chair across the room to give him as a pillow. Nate settled into the couch with a sigh. Sometime since Walter had first brought him into this room, he'd taken Nate's jacket and his pants and boots, and had found a sheet for him to lie on. The sheet was folded in half, the edge tucked between the couch cushions, the loose end snugged tightly around Nate's body in true military fashion. Nate pulled the sheet up to his shoulders for the feeling of security and nothing else.

"You're good at that," he acknowledged out of nowhere. The once-stunning pain had faded to a lion-sized ache.

"Good at what?" Walter asked. Without Nate quite remembering how it had happened, Walter was across the room again, crunching his knees to his chin as he curled up on the love seat. Nate squinted and looked outside, but it only seemed late afternoon. *But then, this boy stayed awake with you all last night. He probably needs a nap.*

"Taking care of me," Nate said, wondering if this was a hard concept for the boy to understand.

"I took care of the animals on the farm back home," Walter said through a yawn. "And my little sister."

"What a good boy," Nate said, falling back to sleep now that some of the pain was alleviated.

"I'm eighteen," Walter told him with dignity, and Nate hurt himself with a gasp.

"How can that be?"

"Easy," Walter mumbled, obviously close to sleep. "Turned eighteen in August, joined the army the same day, shipped out in November, captured in January, escaped in February, and here it is, almost April, and it's still not a year since my birthday. Now do me a favor and quit yammering and let a guy get some sleep."

But now Nate felt mournful. *Such a beautiful boy. I wonder what he will look like when he's all man.*

"You need to slow down," he said succinctly. "You will run out of things to do and not make it till twenty."

Walter's laugh, sleepy and confused, was enough to let Nate know he didn't take it seriously, and Nate was able to close his eyes and sleep.

Several more days, several bouts of fever, lots and lots of willow bark tea.

Walter had changed the sheets and done the laundry, and finally, finally, Nate lay tired and dozy but not sick. Walter had pulled the shunt out, and Nate could breathe without help.

It was a glorious, exhausting feeling, and Nate wanted to lie down and enjoy it, except his bladder was calling to him. It made a furtive, whispering sound now, but soon it would not be nearly as kind about expressing its need.

But he didn't want to get up yet, because he would need help, and he didn't want to wake Walter.

Morning sun made its way through the boards on the windows and illuminated his companion's face. Eighteen—young—and terrifyingly resourceful. He'd applied himself to Nate's convalescence with an astounding single-minded resolve. The abandoned house in the woods gave them many amenities—Nate would be the first to recognize that without shelter and clean water he would have been better off staying in the plane and hoping for rescue before he stopped breathing.

But Walter had nursed him through the fever, fed him broth made from old salt and a new rabbit, and brought him an empty can to piss in. He'd wiped down Nate's body, giving an efficient, welcome sponge bath. Once, when Nate could smell his own sweat so strongly it troubled his stomach, Walter had washed his hair using warm water and some soap he'd found in the bathroom cupboard. Nate could still smell the perfume on the milled soap, and he hadn't sweat as much since the bath, so the smell remained comforting.

He'd laughed with Nate, as well—or at him—but then, Nate remembered being foolish often in the throes of the fever. But the fever was gone, and he was no longer foolish. Tired, and his body ached but not excruciatingly so. He wasn't foolish, only a little bit in awe.

"What're you looking at?" Walter muttered, rolling to his side to talk to him. "You been burning holes in me for about five minutes now."

Nate grimaced. The man was admirable, but he was also blunt.

"I have to relieve myself," Nate said with some embarrassment. "I would rather use the washroom than the mason jar, if that is all right with you."

Walter grunted and swung his legs around to sit up. "That's fair enough. But I been using outside. There's still an old outhouse there. They had a running water line to the bathroom, but it's been turned off—water closet doesn't flush."

Nate blinked and smiled slightly. "What *is* this place?" he mused.

"I been thinking about that," Walter said, standing up and stretching. He wore pants, tailored for someone much taller and larger than he was, with suspenders to keep them up, and he had folded the cuffs multiple times and tacked them, probably with the surgical thread he'd used to stitch Nate. They seemed to float around his small waist, almost like clown pants. Nate eyed the boy critically, wondering if watching his own mother tailoring his clothes was enough to give him the expertise to fix Walter's. Walter stretched his hands over his head then, in a curiously catlike gesture, and the knit undershirt he was wearing hugged what appeared to be a trim, almost-gaunt little body.

Walter lowered his arms and grinned at Nate, not abashed in the least at another man's regard. "I'm scrawny, I know it." He smirked. "I got the body of a turnip in a drought, or that's what . . ." His smirk faded, and he swallowed. "That's what Jimmy used to say." It had cost him to finish his sentence. "Sorry. Didn't mean to get sad on you."

"Not at all," Nate murmured. "There is no shame, I think, to miss a friend."

Walter glanced at him sharply. "That sounded all Jewish and stuff. Is that like . . . like a saying or a proverb or something?"

Nate searched his mind. "No, I don't think so. I think it's mostly common sense."

That grin came back, stretching Walter's cheeks, making him look about ten years old. "Well, it's good sense, but it sounds awfully damned Jewish."

Nate grinned back and sat up creakily. He envied Walter's scrawny body and the ease with which he moved. "I take it you haven't met many Jews."

"In Beauchamp, Iowa? Are you kidding? Indians, yeah, we got some of them, but they mostly stay on the reservation." Walter's face fell. "Seemed a shame. There's a bunch of kids near us when I was growing up. Liked to play stickball. My dad was a real bastard to 'em, but they let me play anyway, when I could get away from him. So, like, I heard about the Jews getting shut up in ghettos, and I thought about them kids on the reservation, except not ever getting to come out. They were nice kids." He smiled uncertainly at Nate, as though he wasn't sure how this bit of information would be taken.

"I'm jealous," Nate said, because honesty had served him well thus far with Walter. "You had peers. Children to play with. I was always . . ." *Too shy. Too different. Too Jewish for the goyim, not Jewish enough for the Jews. Too afraid of looking too long at the wrong person.* "Alone," he said after that pause.

Walter grimaced. "Yeah, well, I'll bet you wish you could be alone to take a leak, don't you? C'mon, let's go."

It was the first time Nate had been outside—or even on his feet—since Walter had brought him here. As Walter shoved his bony shoulder under Nate's arm and made himself available as a human crutch, Nate was struck by how much he *didn't* know about this area where they had crashed. Of course, Nate had spent his entire life in the city, and he had no experience with the closely wooded area in Moselle.

"It's pretty," Nate observed, leaning heavily on Walter. He'd learned in the past days that Walter was surprisingly sturdy.

"Yeah. Iowa's a lot of flat. This felt like something special."

"I was not expecting the heat." Not with so many trees, that was for certain.

"I'm not sure if it's seasonal, or if the woods are just dense, or if there's a factory nearby," Walter confessed. "But it was cold and snowy when I first got here. I'm sort of grateful for the heat."

The old-fashioned outhouse was back behind the house, far enough away so the smell wouldn't bother the inhabitants, close enough to not get lost in the woods on your way to take a piss. There was a garage nearby, with the door closed and green paint peeling from the sides.

"Is there a car, you think?" Nate asked, pausing to breathe heavily. Healing. He was still healing. For a moment, he felt a pressing sense of urgency. They were behind enemy lines, and he was wounded. Didn't he have to get back? Shouldn't he try to unite with . . . somebody? But he could barely walk, and he couldn't think outside the pain and the curiosity, and the gratitude for Walter's sturdy companionship.

"No, I checked. Car's gone. But there's preserves in there on shelves. Lots of fruit. Between that and the wildlife, I've been eating okay."

Nate thought about it. "Is there an orchard nearby? A garden?"

Step, drag, step, drag—soon, very soon, he would be inside the outhouse and able to piss. He looked forward to it.

"Yeah," Walter said shortly. "I passed one on my way here. I . . . Here we are."

Yes, indeed, there they were at the outhouse. But Walter had broken off and hadn't finished that sentence, and Nate was curious why. But now was not the time. The stairs were painstaking, one and two, and then he was in the small room, gasping, holding on to the sides. Walter reached around him, very professionally, and pulled the drawstring on his underwear, then eased them down.

"You need to turn around, and once you're seated, I'll shut the door," Walter said matter-of-factly. "There's some sort of ladies' lingerie catalog there, and a cloth and a small bowl of water—use that however you need. I'll be getting preserves from the garage so give a holler when you're done, okay?"

Nate turned around painfully and sat down, grateful that it appeared as though the lacquered wooden seat had been cleaned and the inside of the outhouse was not too full. There were enzymes, he recalled, that you could put in such a thing. He wondered if Walter had found them in the auto shed as well.

Once he was situated, Walter shut the door, leaving Nate in the darkness. He waited a moment for his body to catch up with his circumstances and listened as Walter stomped to the garage, making, it felt like, more noise than necessary. He was doing that for Nate.

Nate laughed a little. The clumsy stomping was so very Walter. Blunt, no nonsense, but unapologetically careful of his companion's feelings. You probably always knew where you stood with Walter.

Hector would like Walter, Nate thought, and his thoughts paused right there.

Would he? Well, Hector and Joey seemed to get along pretty well, and it was not unheard of for a squad to have four men.

What was he thinking? Why would Hector need to like Nate's new friend? The odds were, if they ever found the Allied forces again, they would probably be shipped to different parts of the war. They could reunite afterward, perhaps, although Nate didn't see Walter walking the streets of New York.

Of course, he didn't see Walter intimidated by them, either.

He was immersed in that thought, Walter stomping through the garment district, shopping and haggling with shopkeepers, when his body remembered how to function. Relieved, he washed up and called out briefly, aware that whatever errands Walter had been running had been completed. The only sound in the tiny, three-by-three building with plain wood walls was Nate's breathing.

"I'm here." Walter's voice came from the other side of the door. "Can you get your pants by yourself or do you need help?"

Embarrassingly enough, Nate needed help. Walter opened the door and reached down to Nate's ankles to get his undershorts, pausing for a moment as he pulled them up.

"Excuse me, mister, but I hope you don't mind me asking you what in the hell happened to your peter?"

Nate choked out a laugh. "Circumcision," he said, shocked and mortified. "To symbolize our covenant with Abraham."

"Well, you 'bout cut off one of my favorite bits! When does *that* happen?"

Nate blushed as Walter finished tying his shorts and then helped him advance, very carefully, down the steps.

"I was a baby," Nate said, still embarrassed. "The mohel comes, there's a bris and a party. It's a way of welcoming the little boy into the world."

Walter's eyebrow was raised in disbelief. Nate was starting to think of that little arch as Walter's "no bullshit" line. It helped that this was something Walter himself would say.

"That's a hell of a welcome," Walter said, sounding genuinely distressed. "Hey, little guy, welcome to the world! We're gonna clip the hood off your pecker! What do they do for girls?" He shuddered. "Never mind. I don't want to know!"

Nate was forced to laugh again, even though the trip to the outhouse had exhausted him. "I think they just put bows in their hair," he said, hoping that would make Walter feel better. "I can't believe you've never seen a circumcised *schmekel* before!"

Walter glared at him, even as they continued to walk, painstakingly, back to the house. "I try really hard not to check out other men's equipment," he said grimly. "First day of basic, Jimmy told me if you check out other men's equipment too closely, they're likely to try to fix you with it, if you know what I mean."

Nate gasped, shocked. "That's horrible!"

"That's the *army*!" Walter replied. "Hell, that's being the little guy. You just don't look too close and don't mention what's different or it's gonna be shoved up your ass right quick!"

Ouch. Nate winced, the idiom being particularly apt. "I guess it is easier to break that rule when you are dealing with an invalid," he remarked sourly, and it was Walter's turn to wince.

"Well, truth be told, I noticed when I was giving you a sponge bath when you were half out of your head, but, well, it didn't seem polite to say anything until now."

A rusty chuckle broke through Nate's reserve. "That's . . . that's really very odd," he said after a couple of moments. They reached the house, and Nate leaned against the side and panted while Walter opened the door and came back down the two steps to help him up. "I'm afraid that's the end of my strength. Wonderful. Should the Vichy forces or the Nazis come bursting down the woods, I can hobble to the outhouse. It is always good to have an escape."

"Don't have to worry about them coming back," Walter said, and for some reason, in the quiet, Nate was peculiarly aware of the heat of that wiry little body next to his. With a grunt, Walter helped him across the sitting room and turned to let Nate sit down. To Nate's surprise, Walter plopped right down next to him. Nate leaned back and turned his head sideways, the better to examine his unlikely savior.

"Why not?" Nate asked, not liking the sound of *coming back*.

Walter turned his head sideways and peered at him, making another picture in Nate's mind. Those eyes were the color of the sea around Greece—so blue and green, they hurt Nate's heart.

"They came by looking for me right after I got here. There's a space between the closet and the wall upstairs—where they made it bigger to fit pipes. I hid up there. They kicked the door in, broke the windows, left. Guess I was lucky they didn't have the dogs, but then, the dogs were somewhere else."

Nate breathed deeply, thought carefully about whether or not this was the time to ask the question. "Walter, how *did* you get here?"

Walter's face tightened, the flesh around his eyes crinkling, and he stood up abruptly, leaving Nate feeling the empty place where he'd sat.

"We still got some stew from the rabbit, but I think I'll go bring up some preserves. They got that sort of pickled cabbage that's a little sour, but in the two-day stew, I think it'll be perfect." Walter turned back toward the door, and Nate watched him about to run away to fetch yet another jar of preserves to match the three already on the counter.

"Walter!"

He paused, his hand on the doorknob, his chest pumping like he'd just been running instead of sharing a curious moment of intimacy. In that heartbeat, neither of them spoke, and Nate realized it was on him to give Walter a reason to confide.

"This is war, and outside this house in the middle of nowhere— the world is insane. I don't know if anything you've done can't be made right."

"All I did was live," he muttered, and then he slid, like a fish, out the front door.

Nate made himself comfortable, leaning back against the corner of the couch in his underdrawers and T-shirt. He was bored—the little trip to the outhouse had tired him out, but he was not ready to sleep just yet. Were there any books upstairs? A deck of cards would be nice. There was another room attached to the sitting room—would there be a library there? The thought of walking across the floor was unbearable. He would have to ask Walter.

He had just—in spite of his best intentions—closed his eyes and started to doze when Walter returned, clattering in with an armload of disparate objects. Without ceremony, he dumped half of them on the love seat he'd been sleeping on and took the rest—jars of the pickled cabbage and some beans, it appeared—into the adjoining kitchen. He'd already put the GI rations he'd scavenged from the plane into the cupboards, but Nate got the feeling he was saving them for a day when rabbits weren't plentiful and the preserves in the garage ran out.

While Walter clunked around the kitchen, making enough noise to discourage conversation, Nate eyed the contents of the love seat with interest.

There were a couple of books—probably written in French, but Nate knew enough from school to at least sharpen his skills—but no deck of cards. There was also a box full of candles and a rudimentary candleholder, the kind a child would make out of clay.

Nate swallowed, realizing, finally, where they might be.

"A summer home," he said abruptly. "This is a summer home—people who had a home in the city but came here to be in the country. Perhaps there's a lake nearby."

There was a final crash, and Walter spoke up. "Why would they take the pictures and the art off the walls?"

Nate had thought of that too. "Because they came here to hide before they left for good. They had probably been selling the art for money—knew the occupation was coming and left."

Walter paused, a cook pot and metal spoon in his hand. "It's a real nice place. I can't believe someone would have a place like this and then another one in the city. Are you sure?"

Nate nodded. "Yes—of course. My parents still take me to a resort in the Catskills one month a year. We swim, play games, put on silly theater. It is a nice place. I suppose if we were better off, we'd have a place like this one, of our own."

Walter grunted and slammed the cook pot down. "Well la-di-da!" he snapped, sounding petulant. "Ain't that nice to have a place for the summer."

Ah. Walter was touchy about being poor. That was uncomfortable, since Nate had never considered himself to be rich.

"What did you do in the summer?" Nate asked, hoping maybe this question would put Walter in a better frame of mind.

"Milked cows and picked squash, along with my mom and old man," Walter said sourly. "But"—some of his frantic activity eased—"we would usually make it to the swimming hole at night. That was nice. You know, getting all clean?" He sighed. "I wonder if I could find the water main. I *miss* showers."

"A lake would be good too," Nate said mildly, "if there is one." He was unprepared for the miserable look Walter sent him.

"I crossed the lake on the way here," he mumbled. "Swam it in January. It's too close to the town and *really* too close to the train tracks. We don't want to go near the lake."

Nate nodded, digesting this information. "How far away *is* it?" he asked politely, because that was good information to know.

Walter shook his head. "I got no idea. I was . . ." He shrugged. "I fell asleep in that cubby while the damned Nazis were in the house. Thought, *Hell, they're gonna shoot me if they find me; I wouldn't mind missing that.* Woke up and they were gone. Was the last time I heard another human soul until your plane went down."

Nate squinted. "So, two months? That's a long time!"

Walter nodded and turned back to finessing the picky stove—this time, with less noise.

"Yeah. Well, I'm just lucky you turned out to be good company, even half out of your head."

"You really are charmed, you know," Nate said, wishing for one of the books to leaf through. "I could have died and my captain could have survived. That would have been no fun at all!"

Walter stood and grunted, apparently satisfied that the stew would warm and he could leave it for a moment. "You want one of them books?"

"Please." Nate smiled gratefully. "I can read some French. Maybe after dinner, I can translate."

Walter's face lit up like fireworks or a sunrise on water. "You could do that?" He put the three books on Nate's lap, and Nate picked up the first one and started leafing through it. "Man, I've been 'bout losing my mind. They don't even have any *cards* here!"

Nate had a sudden thought, and then he grimaced. "I think there's some back in the plane . . . but they're under Captain Albert's seat in the cockpit."

Walter grimaced too. "Well, you been here about a week. Give it another two or three, and by the time you're ready to walk with me there, the animals will have taken care of most of him and we can bury the rest. That'll be good though. It'll be nice to have some cards!"

And so much for Captain Albert Thompson. Nate contemplated feeling bad. If it had been Hector or Joey, he would have. There was just something so vile about using your last breath to curse the person whose lot you shared; Nate was going to have to work harder at forgiveness, that was for certain.

"It will indeed," is what he said. Then he recognized some of the woodcut drawings in the book and smiled happily. "We're in luck! Children's adventure stories—all three volumes. These shall be *very* entertaining, and they might not strain the boundaries of my prep school French too badly either!"

"I can't believe you speak a whole other language," Walter grumbled, taking one of the books from Nate's lap and thumbing through it. "And these are really fancy. Leather covers, gold edging on the page. You'd think they would have tried to sell these too!"

Nate opened the book he was holding to the plate and read the inscription: "'To Jean-Claude on your twelfth birthday. You are never too old for adventure.'" He glanced up at Walter, knowing the expression on his face was soft. "They were probably hoping maybe they would return," he said. "Books are hard to carry and less easy to sell. That's why they hid them in the garage—if they ever returned, perhaps their son's keepsakes would be there."

Walter nodded soberly. "There was a dolly there too. I left her because, you know, two grown men. But . . . I dunno. I think maybe she's lonely." He studied the other side of the room. "Silly—I'm sorry. It's just—"

"No," Nate said quickly. "Go get her. She will make the place less empty. We can put her on the mantel."

Walter grinned. "Will do. I'll be back before the stew heats up." Then, as though he'd thought of this before but had rejected the idea, he added, "There's some clothes out there. I brought the underthings from the garage in case you wanted to wear some, and the clothes I been wearing are upstairs. You can tell I adapted some of the suits and all. But I still need to change your dressings, and you're mostly using the sheets and blankets anyway—"

Nate nodded and realized that Walter was asking for consent. Nate had been undressed for probably three or four days, wearing some poor gentleman's borrowed underclothes, and Walter was hoping that would continue to be acceptable.

"Yes," Nate said. "I understand. I will probably make free use of those clothes at a later date, but you don't need to bring them all in now."

Walter grinned. "Wonderful. I'm about done with running back and forth today, if you must know the truth."

He bounded out of the house, leaving Nate to pore through the book but not before he had the thought that Walter could probably run circles around the house and garage without pausing for breath.

Perhaps he likes looking at me?

Nate felt the flush traveling from his bare feet, up his hairy shins and thighs, and eventually crawling across his stomach, chest, and neck. His entire body tingled, and he ignored all of that and concentrated on the words in front of him. Whether Walter liked to look at him or not, it did not change the fact that Nate was willing to remain in what amounted to his pajamas for another week at the least.

DOLLS ON THE SHELF

Poor dolly. She sat on the mantel looking sad, her porcelain face remote and alien, as Nate read to an avid Walter for the next two weeks.

Nate, bored and willing to spend time reading the books and practicing his own wording so his translations were exciting, would gaze on her sometimes while he was thinking. In the background, he could hear the various domestic sounds as Walter brought in wood and pumped water into jars and bottles to use to wash clothes, and basically did all of the hard housekeeping jobs that most men eschewed doing. Walter, trapped in this house when there was snow on the ground, had been doing these things for himself for months; he apparently wasn't stopping now just because there was another person to care for.

"She's perfect," Nate mused one day when Walter was hanging clothes on a rack that he'd found in the garage. "Her dress is silk and linen, the bows are all hand trimmed—she's exquisite."

"Yeah, so?" Walter was, apparently, scrubbing the dried blood from the clothes Nate had worn when he crashed. Nate watched him as he picked up the trousers, and had a thought.

"Check the pockets. There's a roll of film in the cargo pocket on the side that I think is important."

"Why?" Walter asked. "Wouldn't they send someone else to take the pictures you didn't get back with?"

Ouch. There was nothing like being expendable. "There are not so many of us as you might think," Nate said, trying to hide his hurt. "They had to outfit special planes to fly recon, and only a few men that started in the service qualified to work the cameras. And I wasn't using the plane cameras; my job was night photography, and you need a handheld with a special lens—"

"Sorry, sorry!" Walter held the trousers in one hand and held the other hand up in surrender. "I'm checking—see? There's your film canister. I don't know what you think you're going to do with it, but someday, I'm sure it'll come in handy."

He set the little metal screw-topped canister on the counter and submerged the torn, blood-soaked trousers in the basin of warm, soapy water he'd put in the sink.

"Thank you," Nate said ruminatively. Something about that night, about the timing, about taking those pictures and then being ambushed by too many enemies to clear away from. He was pretty sure the candle had alerted the air recon teams, but he wondered what those recon teams were protecting.

He had the feeling it was something pretty damned important. It had been worth throwing all those planes into a chase and a possible dogfight. They had no idea what was waiting for them as Nate's plane had fled—for all the Jerries had known, Nate and Albert were leading them into an ambush, even though it was only luck that there really had been Allied planes as backup. The point was, that had been an awful lot of firepower against one lone reconnaissance plane when the stakes were so high.

"So what were you saying about the dolly?" Walter asked, like he was trying to make up for being so stubborn.

"She wasn't the girl's best doll," Nate said, looking at the craftsmanship again.

"She looks pretty fancy to me."

"She is. She's perfect. But she wasn't the girl's favorite."

"What makes you say that?"

Nate smiled, remembered the wooden truck that Zev had clutched even as the influenza had taken him. It hadn't been his newest toy, but it had been his most beloved.

"Because a child's best toy is the most ragged. It's like these books. The little boy probably took one favorite book, one favorite car. The little girl probably took a softer dolly, something threadbare from too much hugging. So poor dolly—the second best dolly. She gets to see all the action, all the things left behind, but she's not the most loved by far."

Walter's face did something complicated then—wrinkled over his eyebrows and at the bridge of his nose. "That's sad," he said, his voice throbbing with empathy for a doll on a shelf. "That must be rough, wanting to be the rag doll, wishing you were the ragged thing, when all you did wrong was be too perfect."

Nate smiled at him, almost wanting to console him. "Yes, well, we shall have to be entertaining company of the first water, so that she doesn't notice she is the consolation prize."

Walter shook his head and waved his hand, blowing away Nate's fancy for the nonsense it was, but later, Nate would remember that doll of all things and think of his beloved Carmen. Poor doll. It was not her fault she was everything that was perfect when the owner of her heart wanted everything that was not.

"Are you translating?" Walter demanded grumpily into the rather melancholy silence that had fallen. "Because I know I didn't let you up to help today, but you got one job, and that's to keep me from being bored out of my fricking mind."

"You know, I'm a soldier too. You *can* say 'fuck' around me." He'd noticed that since their conversation about summer homes, Walter seemed to try to mind his manners around Nate. It was both sweet and embarrassing. It made Nate feel soft. Coming up through basic training, the other men had sworn as much as possible to try to get under Nate's skin, but he'd gotten good at ignoring them. This? It felt like he was being mollycoddled.

"I'm *trying* to be a gentleman," Walter snapped, and Nate stared at him in amazement.

"A gentleman?"

"Lookit you, translating French, talking about summer places—"

"We didn't have one!"

"You didn't have a swimming hole and a barn full of cow shit, either," Walter muttered. "Maybe, just maybe, I don't want to be someone less than you. You ever think of that?"

Nate stared at him, feeling completely off-kilter. "You dragged me out of a plane and cared for my wounds, Walter. How elitist do you think I will be?"

"I don't want you to pity me. I'm not a real doctor, and I got no education. So maybe I just want to not be a redneck in front of you, you think maybe?"

Nate didn't point out that he'd just said *maybe* twice. "I didn't know it bothered you," he mumbled.

"You're an *officer*," Walter told him—something Nate had known but hadn't really made much of.

"But I didn't earn that in battle," he said, trying to smile like the ineffective fop he knew himself to be. "I sat in the plane, took pictures, and hung on while the real hero did all the flying. There was no battle, no promotion. I knew how to take pictures, how to take care of the field equipment. I didn't storm the beach in Africa or even fire a shot that killed anybody. There's no reason to think all that much of me—"

"God, you're stupid," Walter muttered, but he sounded resigned when he said it, which was better than irritated.

"I just don't understand why it matters one way or the other whether you say 'fuck' in front of me."

"It fucking doesn't," Walter said flatly, and then held up the wet trousers.

"Not bad!" Nate praised. "Not felted or shrunk, and you seem to have gotten all of the blood out. When they dry, I shall try to stitch them, and they shall be wearable again."

"Do you sew?" Walter asked quizzically.

"I watched my mother when I was a boy. I think I've learned a few things."

Walter made an indeterminate noise then—sort of a thoughtful grunt. He had an entire collection of what Nate was starting to think of as "old man" sounds. So much about Walter was older than his actual age. "Nothing you just said makes me think I should swear in front of you, do you know that?"

Nate narrowed his eyes. "Walter, when the fucking trousers are dry, if you give me a fucking needle and thread, I will fucking sew the hell out of them."

Walter started to laugh then, an evil chuckle. He didn't say much else for a few moments, just kept up that slightly insane sound while he moved on to Nate's flight jacket and some of the dusty underclothes he'd recovered from the garage.

Nate went back to reading a children's story, wherein the boy who obeyed his parents was able to adventure out in the big scary world and survive with his morals intact. Nate was not aware that he made a sound until Walter broke into his thoughts.

"How bad could it be? That Jean-Simone character didn't get his foot shot off or anything, did he?"

"No— What? My God, that's morbid!"

"Then what was that sigh about?"

Nate wrinkled his nose, rattled. Among many other complexities, it appeared Walter was also quite perceptive.

"It just seems very convenient, doesn't it, that the answer to all of poor Jean-Simone's problems is to obey his father. I personally would prefer *not* to obey my father. My father hasn't spoken five words in a row to me since my brother died. I told him I was shipping out for boot camp, and do you know what he said?"

"'Fucking eat breakfast there'? Because that's what *my* father said."

Nate recoiled. "Why would he tell you to eat breakfast at boot camp?"

"He didn't want to give me the food. It was three days by bus. Last thing I did before I left home was steal a loaf of bread and a jar of peanut butter so I didn't starve."

"Well, that . . . that makes my father look like a paragon of charity, actually. My God, Walter. What did your mother say?"

Walter shook his head. "Just that she'd rather me get blown up than turn out queer."

Nate gasped. "That's . . . Why would she say that?"

Walter turned his back and started to concentrate on the laundry. When he spoke, his voice was garbled and defensive. "Isn't that how *all* mother's think?"

Nate closed his eyes and tried to imagine what his mother would say if he confessed that fizzy, happy, golden feeling he got when he looked at Hector Garcia. Or Walter. Especially Walter.

Which would be worse? That he's a man or that he's goyim?

The thought made him laugh. "I think for my mother, she'd rather a Jewish man than a gentile woman. But then, that is my mother." It was a lie, relying on the stereotype of his people, but it was worth telling, worth pretending the words didn't hit home, just to hear that evil giggle as it shook Walter's shoulders again.

"Lucky you," he said, but he no longer sounded defensive and upset. "So, you never did say . . . What did your father say when you told him you were shipping out?"

Nate closed his eyes and tried to do a good impersonation of Selig Meyer. "'What? The world needs one less Jew?'"

Walter made another one of those old-man sounds. "What in the hell is that supposed to mean?"

"I don't think he thought enough of me to believe I'd survive."

"Yeah?"

"You don't think so?"

Walter shrugged. "I don't know. I think it sounds worried. Like he didn't want you to go because he was afraid for you."

"You got that, from seven words?"

"Well, you're the one who said them. If you said them right, then yeah. I think that's exactly what he was thinking."

"Oh." Absurdly, Nate felt near tears. "Well then."

Walter sighed, put one more thing in the basin, and then dried his hands on a towel he'd scrounged from somewhere and came to sit down at Nate's feet.

"I'm sorry," he said, his voice soft as he leaned back against the couch. "I didn't mean to make you sad. You know, I found flour in the stores. There's a sifter too. I could get some of the weevils out and see about maybe making us some bread. What do you think?"

"Yeast?" Nate wouldn't quibble with the idea of bread on any day.

"No." Walter's face fell. "I guess all that would make is a cracker."

"Boil it," Nate said. "Knead it until it's tough, then boil it before you bake it. Maybe the yeast won't matter so much. That's how some bagels are made."

"How *what* are made?"

Nate blinked at him. Well, true—he'd already *said* he didn't know any Jews.

"Bagels. They're sort of round, chewy bread."

Walter smiled, wide and delighted. Nate realized he was missing some teeth in the back, but not even that could mar the joy of that smile. "That there is a terrific idea. I'll have to go see if I can make us some bagels."

"If you put them on a tray after they're done and toast them, they get nice and golden brown."

Walter went to slap Nate's leg in excitement and then, apparently, remembered that Nate was recovering. He paused, let his hand come down softly, and then stayed there, looking at his hand as though he could find some way to take away the awkwardness.

"That's a good idea," he said quietly, apparently relieved when Nate peered up and smiled.

"You'll get home," Walter said with confidence. "You'll get better. We'll find a way to hook you up with your squad again. They'll be missing you."

"What about you?" Nate asked, not wanting to talk about the coldly written letter under his pillow. Would they have sent it by now? Or was he still MIA? *Did they send the letters when you were MIA?* Nate had never asked.

"They probably assumed I was dead in Africa," Walter said thoughtfully. "They took prisoners in Morocco. Shipped us by train. I mean, I gave them my intel—name, rank, serial number—but they didn't take me too seriously. Kept laughing, calling me *verkleinem*. I think it meant runt."

The camera in Nate's mind clicked again: Walter's battered, capable hand flexing over the cover, and there he was, touching Nate through the sheet, no awkwardness, no hesitation. He was simply lost in his story.

Nate would not call his attention to that hand for all the world.

"So you were shipped to Germany on a train?" Nate asked, and Walter clenched his hand and shuddered.

"Yup. Train wrecked. Bunch of us took advantage of the wreck—we were starving, anyway." His voice sank. "The German doctor was always nice to me. I hit him in the face with the butt of a guard's rifle and took his medical bag."

Oh.

"That was good thinking."

"The captain got shot. The one in our car as we were getting away. I . . ." Walter took a breath, and Nate wished he could lean forward and grab his hand. Who did that? Who grabbed another man's hand? *She would rather I got blown up than come back queer.* Was that a hint?

A truth? Walter was small—his heart-shaped face held a sweet sort of beauty. His father sounded . . . well, awful. Was it just an assumption? Walter wasn't big enough to *be* a bully, so he must be queer?

"I tried to haul him with me," Walter said in a small voice. "You see it in the movies, the one soldier not letting the other go. We got into the woods, and he was dragging me down and dying, and they were coming after us, with dogs. He told me to go. I didn't even have time to run. I left him at the base of a tree and climbed up. I . . ."

He clutched Nate instinctively through the sheet, and Nate was going to do it, seize his hand, give him comfort, when suddenly he stood up, pushing off Nate's foot and stomping to the other side of the room.

"He didn't make it," Walter said, his voice remote. "But I did, and I kept running. Held on to the damned bag the whole way. It was like . . . like . . . I lost my unit, and they made me a medic. I couldn't lose that or who else would I be?"

He turned to Nate then, his mouth moving for a moment, and his gaze bleak. "So, see? You're expected. You've got a place to go. Nobody even cares I'm alive."

He made it back to the kitchen and continued to wash clothes, and Nate watched him with troubled eyes.

"I do," he said into the sudden silence. "I know you're alive."

Walter didn't look at him. "Be sure to tell your grandchildren about me, then. I bet it'll be a great story."

What shall I tell them, Walter? That you touched my leg and my body tingled? That's not something you tell your grandchildren.

"I'll be sure to tell them about your kindness and your resourcefulness, as well," Nate said, keeping his voice neutral. Walter glanced up briefly and met his eyes.

"That would be nice of you," he said, sincerity dripping from his words.

"Well, yes. I live to be nice." The words sounded bitter, and they rang in the empty room as the late-afternoon sunshine heated the air, because apparently neither of them had anything else to say after that.

The silence healed after dinner. Walter had set another rabbit snare, as well as discovered the early volunteer carrots from what was probably a summer garden, and the resulting stew was quite tasty. Nate wondered if they would ever get to the GI rations they'd snagged from the plane, and if not, why had Walter even asked for them? It would occur to him later that like so many during the Depression, Walter had been used to living in want. There was no such thing as enough food when there had been no food at all for so long.

Nate read another adventure story, and Walter sat on the floor, knees drawn to his chest, hanging on every word. This story was about a trip to the ocean and a runaway boat. The young, intrepid hero swam to the boat and rescued the small children who had disobeyed their parents and drifted away. (Nate had to work hard at not rolling his eyes at this part. Walter didn't care about the subtext; he just wanted a happy ending.) When Nate got to the end of the story, he looked at Walter, with his shining eyes and quiet delight. His mental camera took the shot when he wasn't paying attention, and he rethought his earlier cynicism.

"You like the story?" he asked needlessly, and Walter nodded.

"I was worried there for a minute. It's hard to be brave."

"Yes," Nate agreed. "But then, you are very brave, so you would know."

"Don't talk down to me," Walter said abruptly, standing up. "Blow out the candle."

Nate did and heard the sounds of Walter stripping to his undershorts and T-shirt, and hanging the pants and jacket over the back of the love seat. Sometime during Nate's fever, he had moved a sheet and a blanket down in order to sleep in the same room.

"It is kind of you," Nate said into the dark, "to stay down here and keep me company. I haven't seen the upstairs, but the mattress must be nicer."

"It's not bad," Walter acknowledged. Moonlight penetrated the slats between the window boards. Nate could make out Walter, sliding between the sheets. "But it's good to hear someone else breathing under the same roof, you know?"

"Yes," Nate conceded. "I do."

Walter made puppy sounds then, curling up on the love seat and resting his head, and Nate closed his eyes, still healing, his own head on the uncomfortable bolster. Dreamy, half-asleep, he said, "I wish you had a pillow."

"Thanks, Nate. I'll wish a pillow for you too."

And Nate fell asleep dreaming about their heads, together, on the same pillow.

The dream changed, near morning. A dance at the USO. Joey Shanahan was there with the most beautiful redheaded girl Nate had ever seen, and Joey stared at her, besotted, his narrow, pock-scarred face alight with pure love. Hector was there in his zoot suit, in full-color purple and gold, dancing with his girl, their bodies a frantic whir in the big band jitterbug.

And Walter was there, standing at his side, wiry body dapper in a fine gray suit, turquoise eyes bright with the music and the lights. Nate smiled down at him and held out a hand, and they were dancing, whirling like tornadoes on the dance floor. They spun like a carousel, laughing to the cheering and clapping of the crowd.

The music changed to a Glenn Miller tune, and Walter tucked into his arms, his body aligned to Nate's, and the lights lowered.

Nate gazed into Walter's eyes, and he was glowing, staring at Nate like a hero, and Nate felt like a giant among men.

He awakened abruptly, chest tight with what felt like unshed tears, and looked around. The light outside the boards was the faintly lighter gray of predawn.

"You okay?" Walter asked, closing the door behind him. He was shivering and wiping his hands on the back of his pants as he walked to the kitchen. He kept a basin of soapy water there, always, and used it to wash his hands—apparently again.

"Privy?" Nate asked, blinking hard.

"Yeah. You gotta use it?"

"Probably later," Nate answered with a sigh. He could get up and walk around the room now, but even the half flight of stairs to the bedrooms and the short trip to the outhouse were both a risk still. His body felt tight and uncomfortable from the dream, and he didn't want to stand in case Walter would see.

"Well, you could always go back to sleep."

Nate closed his eyes but didn't obey. The dream was settling into his bones now, settling into his heart. Hector had been happy with his girl, vibrant, alive, and Joey had been too.

And Nate had danced with Walter, close as any man and woman, and his whole body had yearned for that touch, yearned for more. With a struggle, Nate turned to face the back of the couch and brought his knee up to hide his aching and erect flesh.

It was all so much easier when he'd harbored a faint yearning for a man who could not want him back.

The next weeks were a study in getting better. His lung was the slowest thing to heal—his leg and ribs were sore, but simply walking across the room or the wooded yard to the outhouse took all his breath. Still, step-by-step, he built up his health. If nothing else, he didn't want to be a burden to Walter.

He repaired the hole in his trousers, as promised, using the neat, delicate stitches he'd seen his mother use, and Walter whistled low over his shoulder as he'd sewn.

"That there is fancy work," he said with awe. "My ma couldn't do that unless she used a machine."

"Your mother wasn't relying on the trousers to get her through enemy territory to find an Allied outpost, either," Nate said drolly.

Walter's sweet expression of praise dried up. "Do you have to?" he asked, sounding naked. "Do you have to leave?"

Nate shrugged. "Well, not this minute, Walter, but we can't stay here forever. The Nazis or the Vichys—or even the Allies—somebody is bound to stumble across this place. And we don't even have a radio. At this moment, we don't know who's who or what's going on at all. And we're in the woods, aren't we? It's not like another plane is going to crash and give us a clue as to what's going to happen."

"Yeah," Walter muttered. "Yeah, I get it. I just— One army or the other, it felt just the same to me."

Nate held on to his temper and reminded himself that Walter's world had been very small before he'd taken a bus to Fort Dix from Iowa. "Perhaps that is because you're not Jewish."

Walter's silence was offended at first, and then simply thoughtful. "I forget," he apologized. "I mean, I'm white trash—I know it. But I carry that chip on my shoulder, and I forget sometimes there's bigger reasons to be in the war than politicians saying stuff over the radio."

"There are rumors," Nate said lowly, because nobody wanted to talk about this, not at Menwith Hill, not back in the States. "Terrible rumors, about where all the Jews are going. I don't have a gun, but wouldn't it be something if I could help make it stop?"

Walter's hand on his shoulder was both electric and disquieting at once.

"You think so big," he said disconsolately. "My only plan when I signed up was three squares a day. And keeping by Jimmy."

Ah, the elusive and mysterious Jimmy. "Did you sign up with Jimmy?" Nate asked, going back to his stitchery. The dim light in the little front room was at its best this time of day.

"Naw. Met in boot camp. Little guys. Watched each other's backs." Walter's voice buckled. "Best friend I ever had."

"It's good," Nate said carefully, thinking about Hector and Joey. "When you find someone who accepts you for everything you are." Well, not everything, but enough of who he was.

"You try," Walter said, with another of those condescending pats on the shoulder. "But you're smarter. You're an officer. You gotta keep all professional. I know that."

"I'm . . . what?" Nate gaped at him as he walked toward the door. "I . . . I have to what? I have . . ." He flailed the needle Walter had gleaned from an upstairs cabinet. "In what way have I been distant?"

Walter turned the doorknob. "Don't take it wrong, Nate, but you're Lieutenant Nathan Meyer—it says so on the flight jacket you're gonna stitch up next. Don't worry, I never forgot it."

A surge of red washed across Nate's vision, and he shoved himself upright and took two steps toward the door, breathing hard enough to make his ribs and chest ache. When he opened his mouth he was trying to yell, but he didn't have enough wind.

"I have bared my soul to you!" he whisper-shouted, then dragged in a big, painful breath. "What else could I have told you about myself to make you—"

The door slammed, and he staggered back down to the couch. How was he supposed to finish that sentence? He'd thought they'd been growing closer, each and every day. *Make you feel close to me?* Was that what he was going to say? When they'd started out, Walter had no reservations about talking to Nate honestly, but that seemed to have changed. *Make you forget that we're different?* Was that what he wanted?

Oh, come now, Nate. It's an empty room in the middle of the woods. Be honest.

"Love me," he finished aloud, then closed his eyes. Because, of course, the answer was right there. Such a risk—such a terrible, terrible risk—to tell another man he loved him. The only way to let them in was to tell them; the surest way to lose him was to do the same thing. It had never been tempting with Hector.

But then, he and Hector had never been locked in a small house for what was going on a month now, with only tales of their childhoods for company.

When Walter came back in about an hour later, Nate held up the trousers with ironic aplomb.

"They look great," Walter said, not meeting his eyes. "You want to wear them to accompany me to the crash site tomorrow? I'm thinking we can get the radio from the plane. There's outlets here. If you've got a cord, we can maybe listen and see if we can pick up some Allied frequencies."

Nate's face fell. "I'd love to, but . . . I can't even yell from across the room. Maybe a few more days," he said, and Walter's return smile was unaccountably brilliant.

"Two more days is fine," he said. "Tomorrow we can go outside and walk around the house. You can get a feel for the terrain."

"And tonight I'll read some more," Nate said, feeling naked. Walter was making plans for them already. He didn't even want to leave himself, but he was making plans to split up from Nate.

"That's real generous of you, sir," Walter said.

"Don't," Nate said harshly. "For weeks I haven't been 'sir'—don't do that to me now."

"Why not?" Walter asked in a little voice, heading for the kitchen. He'd tried making the bagels, and they hadn't turned out badly. He'd sifted the flour many, many times, so the weevils were few and far between, and they had enough rabbit stock left over to make gravy to sop with the bagels. It was neither a deli in New York nor the KP at Menwith Hill, but Nate had no complaints. Nate watched as Walter moved to wash his hands first and wondered what he was going to do. Toast the bagels? Warm the gravy?

Pull old potatoes out of his pockets and start washing them?

Of course it was the last thing—clever, clever Walter.

"Because I think of you as a friend," Nate said, wanting to thank him and celebrate him. "Calling me 'sir' feels like a slap in the face."

"It helps me remember," Walter mumbled, going for the broken kitchen knife that had been left behind.

"Remember what?"

"That you need to leave, and I'm going to be left alone again."

"We'll get you assigned somewhere when we get back to a unit," Nate said, desperate for Walter to feel remembered.

"Wonderful." Walter concentrated on peeling the potato with the exactness of die-cut machinery.

"Or perhaps you could be transferred to Menwith Hill. I'll be there. We could see each other—"

"Do the officers even talk to the enlisted men?" Walter asked with deep suspicion.

"I'm an officer by accident!" Nate argued, not even sure what he was arguing about. "Please, Walter!"

"Please what?" Walter snapped, forced to raise his face and look Nate in the eyes. "I don't even know what you want from me!"

Your love. For you to not withdraw from me now that I've gotten used to us being close. I don't want you to pull away now.

"Your . . . your friendship," Nate said quietly, fighting not to pull back. "I . . . I enjoy your company. Please . . . we're . . . we're soldiers in the same war, but . . . I *like* you. Ca i't we just deal with each other in that way?"

Walter turned back to the potatoes. "Sure," he said softly. "Sure. But . . . we'd never be friends outside this house. You know that, right, Nate? Me and Jimmy—we coulda met at a grange meeting, or in the drugstore, or at the post office. You and me?"

"We would have met somewhere," Nate said, his heart beating in his throat. He knew—he wasn't stupid. Class differences. Walter *was* poor white trash, not that Nate or even his father would have said that out loud. Where did a middle-class Jewish boy think he was going to meet a Walter. But *oy*! Not to have met Walter? Ever? "I refuse to believe we wouldn't have met in a place where we could be friends. Isn't that what the war is about? Hitler is saying to hate everybody not him, and everybody not him is saying they deserve to be equal?"

Walter grunted. "I thought it was because Hitler is bombing everybody who's not white to powder. What he says is nothing. It's when he starts shedding blood that we need to put that asshole down!"

Of course. There were ideals and there were practicalities. Nate dealt with the first, but Walter? Walter was the one who could cook dinner and breakfast for two grown men given nothing but a sack full of flour, an old winter garden, and a forest full of rabbits.

"What I'm saying," Nate tried once more, "is that there should always be a world in which you and I meet."

Walter's shrug would have done an old uncle at temple proud. "We meet, we don't meet—if we don't know each other, it doesn't make a difference."

But it does. I was missing you before you were born.

The next day, Walter boiled more water and filled one big pot and one big basin with it and added soap. He went into the stores and the painstakingly stocked drawers full of borrowed clothing and came back with two suits, underthings included. Then he spread a mat on the kitchen floor and started to unbutton his shirt while Nate stood and watched, uncomfortable and curious.

"You want to go first or should I? I like the water real, real hot, so I don't mind taking the first shift, but you're gonna need to do my back."

Nate gaped as Walter continued taking off his clothes. He didn't fold them up. Instead, he put them in a small pile that Nate assumed was wash.

"I take it we're bathing?" Nate said through a dry throat. Walter skinned off his undershorts quickly and left them in the pile.

"I am tired of smelling my own privates," Walter said frankly. "And while I can't smell yours yet, I imagine you are tired of smelling yours too."

Nate's entire body was awash with embarrassment. One more surge didn't make any difference. "You have, um, cleaned mine more recently, I would imagine. And I do less to sweat than you do."

"Are you telling me you don't want a bath? Even a GI bath?"

"No," Nate said, trying to keep his breathing even. "Not at all. Proceed."

Without ceremony, Walter squatted down over the basin, naked in the kitchen, and started scrubbing while Nate was torn between looking and not looking, trying to determine which action would make him look less—

Oh God. Even Walter's narrow back, peach and pink colored, with freckles all over his slender shoulders, blocking out anything untoward, rushed the blood to Nate's aching, circumcised cock. All Walter had to do was turn his head and see Nate's rampant erection as it fell down the side of his shorts and he'd know Nate for what he was.

So flamingly, irredeemably queer that just the sight of Walter's pale skin made him hard.

"Your ribs paining you?" Walter asked, casting a glance over his shoulder.

"No," Nate squeaked. "Why?"

"Your breathing went all funny there for a minute." He dipped the washcloth in the still-steaming basin and squeezed the water out, then handed it back over his shoulder to Nate. "Here—get my back and my neck after I stand up, okay? It gets itchy if you don't."

Nate took the cloth automatically and then waited while Walter stood. Firmly, and without fuss, he rubbed the washcloth along Walter's shoulders, trying to ignore the sensual shiver that Walter gave. Standing this close, Nate could smell wet animal, and he had to concede that yes, it had probably been some time since Walter had bathed. But that didn't mean that the smell of the new, cleaner Walter wasn't . . . intriguing . . . all on its own.

Nate slid the cloth down to Walter's lower back, and his heart lodged in his throat.

"What?" Walter turned his head and grinned. "I've got the whitest ass you ever seen, don't I?"

Nate grinned back, supremely conscious of his size and feeling awkward in Walter's personal space in a unique and disturbing way.

"It is a small and shining moon," he said with a wink. "But I'll let you wash that yourself."

Walter shrugged. "I got the creases, nuts, and bolts—it's pretty clean. Here, give me the cloth. I gotta get my pits, and then it's your turn."

Nate tried not to gasp when their fingers met, warm and damp, as Walter swung around and took the cloth. Nate stepped back to rest some of his weight on the counter, and so he could turn a little and disguise his body as it burgeoned.

Walter noticed though, and being Walter, he commented. "The draft in the kitchen got to you, didn't it?" he asked impishly. "Happens." He swiveled his hips, and Nate's eyes were drawn to Walter's cock, pale and growing, as it flopped against his slender thigh.

Oh. Good. They could make this a natural thing, an everyday thing among men, and not Nate's longing to run his darker-skinned hand down Walter's pale skin and to count those myriad peach-colored freckles.

Nate stared forward resolutely and went to skin off his undershorts, but his ribs were still a little sore and the shorts caught on his foot. Walter bent to help him out, and the sight of Walter's head that close to his naked groin made his supposedly "natural" condition pulse a little harder.

Walter jumped back, startled, and then grinned up at him like a little kid. "Hel*lo*, Little Nathan, and aren't you happy to see me!"

"Thrilled," Big Nathan said, mortified. "Now let me have the cloth."

"Here, let me get your back first," Walter said, "and then I can get dressed so Little Walter ain't flapping around in the breeze."

"Very wise," Nate said, wondering how this moment could possibly get longer or more awkward.

Then Walter started scrubbing his back, and Nate closed his eyes and prayed for it to continue a little longer.

The cloth swooped down the back of his neck, soaking the hair there that was growing long enough to curl, and then across his shoulders, the warm water being left to dry on his newly clean skin. His shoulders did that surprisingly sensual shiver he'd seen Walter's do, just from the joy of not having sweat clinging to his skin anymore.

"You're right," Nate told him, eyes rolling in appreciation. "It feels wonderful to be clean."

"Yeah? Wait till you get to your privates—that's the best part."

Nate nodded and smiled, and grabbed the side of the tile counter and began to lower himself slowly, not sure if his thighs could hold a squat long enough to clean himself down there.

"Crap. Wait a second," Walter said suddenly, hauling on his boxers and then trotting through the house and up the mysterious stairs. He came back with a short stool, which he bent down and set by Nate's foot. "No—don't squat!" he ordered and picked up the basin, careful not to slosh, and set it on the counter.

"That's probably better," Nate admitted, not sure if his body was flushing because he was naked or because Walter had seen how weak he still was.

"Yeah. It'll be even better when I add new water," Walter confirmed. He dumped the water he had used out the open window. There was a bush down there that was growing bigger and faster than anything else in the yard, and now Nate knew why. Within minutes, he had a clean basin filled from the kettle on the stove, and Nate gingerly dipped the rinsed cloth into the steaming water and started to wash.

And yes, it did feel heavenly.

As he swiped the warm water across his chest and his neck, he tilted his head back and gave a sensual sigh.

"How wonderful is this?" he asked rhetorically. "Ah, God, I can see why people go to hot springs now, or sit in saunas. Just the heat alone on the muscles—it's a good thing."

"You're welcome," Walter said decisively, hauling a T-shirt on. Nate watched him out of the corner of his eye, missing his skin as soon as it disappeared. He picked that moment to wash around his genitals, spending as much time as was reasonable on his creases. His cock was clamoring, crying for attention, but he knew better. For one thing, all it would take was a little squeeze, a little stroke, and he would be pleasuring himself in front of this man who had done nothing but be kind to him, and that was embarrassing, even without the other thing. The thing that made it happen in the first place.

His foot was propped up on the little stool, and his weight was on his good knee when a sudden trick of tired muscles made his knee give. He grabbed the counter, and Walter grabbed his elbow, and he bore himself up with Walter's help, his small body pressed against Nate's, and everything—sun, moon, birds outside, Nate's blood and breathing—froze in time as he stood, naked, with another man's hand, however peripherally, touching him.

It was like a current of electricity, arc-welding him in place.

And Walter didn't seem to know a thing.

"Here," he said breezily. "You hold on to the counter, and I'll scrub your calves and shins and such."

He was so humble, Nate thought. Squatting in the kitchen, bathing Nate like a Roman servant. Nate's body was swelling shamelessly, and Walter scrubbed at Nate's hairy shins with cheerful aplomb. In the end, Nate had to close his eyes, close his eyes and remember the last baseball game he'd attended, wearing his service uniform before he shipped out, sitting in the stands by himself wistfully because he hadn't made friends in boot camp and the friends he would make were still half a world away.

His body deflated, and Walter stood up and handed him a bath sheet. The world returned to normal, and he was an awkward, hairy man, standing in an abandoned kitchen.

At least he was clean, eh?

Walter patted him on the back. "Well done, sir. Maybe tomorrow, we can go on a little walk."

"That would be wonderful," Nate said, pretending his smile was natural. "I would dearly love to get out of here."

The hell of it was, he really would. Having Walter so close was killing him.

FOUND IN WRECKAGE

It took him another week before he felt confident enough to go walking toward the plane. He and Walter moved slowly, drinking water from a flask Walter carried and trying not to make as much noise as the finale at a big top circus as they plowed through the undergrowth of the tensely woven forest.

It wasn't hard to find the plane. Although the forest had begun to recover with new growth in the intervening month, the scar from the beheaded treetops still extended for a good half mile. At one of their stops, Walter tilted his head back and surveyed the damage with a low whistle.

"Man, your pilot may have been a son of a bitch, but he sure did know what he was doing in the air!"

Nate had to agree. Looking at that long path in, his heart started a thready tattoo in his throat.

"It's a miracle the plane made it," he said softly, although to prove that God didn't give out miracles at the drop of a hat, they spotted the plane at the next rise.

"You might not want to look," Walter cautioned the moment they made out the dark-gray–painted wooden siding. "I knew he was dead right off. I'm sure the animals did too."

"I should take his dog tags," Nate said quietly. "And if we can, we should bury him."

"Not sure there'll be anything left to bury," Walter said, his customary bluntness in place. "See? You been laid up awhile. I reckon critters made off with the meaty parts and birds pretty much plucked all the wool from his clothes."

What was left was ghastly—a nightmare collection of clean bones and scant scraps of bug-infested flesh. Walter had scavenged work gloves, though, as well as an oilskin bag from the garage, and Nate murmured a blessing over the bones as they transferred them to the bag and then to a quiet place in the forest within sight of the plane.

"What are you singing?" Walter asked after they'd dumped the contents of the sack unceremoniously into a freshly dug hole. Nate fished out the dog tags, as promised, and folded them in his kerchief. Someone would want them. The captain's family had loved him, even if Nate couldn't bring himself to feel much pity.

"A prayer," Nate said. "The Mourner's Kaddish. It's from Ezekiel."

Walter nodded. "Bible things. That's nice. You got any words to say for him?"

Nate shook his head. "I wish I could have mourned him," he said after a moment. "But whether he resented me or no, I'm grateful. He saved my life."

Walter's smile was the first childlike thing Nate had ever seen about him.

"Maybe there's special words for someone who should have been nicer," he said decisively. "It's a real good thing you're doing, singing a blessing for his bones."

Nate sighed, pulled his gloves off, and stood up. They'd brought a camp shovel with them to dig the hole, and now he took his turn filling it in.

"You make me feel like a better person," Nate said honestly. "But that doesn't mean I'm not longing for another sponge bath in the kitchen."

Walter nodded glumly. He'd grabbed the cards from underneath the seat right after they'd moved Captain Thompson's remains, and they both had to admit reaching into the cubby had been a truly unpleasant job. The disheartening thing had been that the cards were all that was left. The radio had been damaged irreparably during the crash. Perhaps Joey or Hector, used to dealing with such equipment all the time, could have repaired it, but not Nate.

"Your camera seems to be okay, though," Walter observed as they pulled out the case.

"That will help us very much, if there's a Nazi outpost we need to bomb," Nate said, trying not to be bitter.

But now, as Walter finished filling in Captain Albert Thompson's grave, Nate couldn't help hoping that the camera would be intact. It might make him feel less useless if he had a weapon to cling to.

"Should we mark it?" Walter asked.

Without a word, Nate took the RAF insignia he'd removed from what was left of Albert's jacket and pushed it into the earth, lodging it against the tree, as well.

"Rest easy, Captain," Nate said quietly, with as much reverence as he could manage. "Your duty's done."

Walter wrapped the shovel in the outside of the oil bag, and together they turned and walked back toward the house.

Nate was stumbling by the time they returned, tripping over the top step into the entryway, and Walter had to grab his elbow and help him to the couch. He'd been silent on the trip back, taciturn and exhausted, and now he glanced up at Walter with a bleakness in his heart he could not ever remember feeling.

"I have no idea," he said. "None. No idea what to do next. The world is going to hell around us. I probably have a mission in that little film canister—something that would help the Allies, even in a small way, but . . . I'm tired, and my French may be better but yours is appalling and we're behind enemy lines where I could be detained for walking down the road just looking Jewish. What do we do? Lurk here like field mice?"

"We eat," Walter said briskly. "I put this back in the garage, and we eat. We change into some of the lounging pants that were out there, and we lounge. You read me the next adventure story, and we see if maybe my French don't get better. We play cards, because I'm betting you're a sure hand at rummy. We sleep. No reason to get all beat down. Peace ain't a bad thing."

He turned and stumped away, and Nate watched him, smiling slightly. *We eat.* Perhaps, tonight, he would help Walter with food and cleanup. It wasn't right Walter should bear the burden for all of—

He fell asleep on the thought.

When he woke up, Walter was browning bagels in the oven, with a nice stew going on the stovetop, and the chill he'd never noticed in the evening was warded off by the wood fire.

And he thought, perhaps, Walter had been right after all.

Walter went out of his way to be charming that night, and even boiled an extra pot of water so they could have a quick wipe down before bed. He moved an old crate in from the mysterious garage, and the two of them played rummy for the length of an entire candle. Nate won, hugely, and then he lost, and would continue to lose most atrociously, for nearly every hand they played together. It took him many years to figure out that while he had been playing numbers and strategy, Walter had been playing *him*, his facial expression, his noises, his grunts in the dark.

When the candle burned down, they made ready for bed, undressing to their underclothes and folding their trousers and shirts over the arms of the couches, and lay down.

"You know," Nate murmured, thinking longingly of the second-floor bed—any bed—because the springs on the couch were weak on his big, healing body, "I think the farthest I'll get tomorrow is upstairs."

"Yeah." Walter's voice sounded remote in the dark. "The bed in the main bedroom is pretty big, has some sheets left still. I think we can share it with not too much problem. It would feel better on the bones, that is for sure."

A pleasant thought, an easy thought. Nate fell asleep to that thought, and on the vague hope that he and Walter would sleep closely, and maybe even touch.

A week passed. Nate's wind grew stronger, and he could help Walter with some of the chores. He could, thank God, make it to the privy by himself without incident. The early spring of March had given way to the hard, bright spring of April, although for a few days, they were confined to the living room while rain pattered all about. There were a few holes in the roof, many of them upstairs, so they stayed on the couches where they would be sure no water would start pouring on their heads in the middle of the night. Nate thought, watching water seep in the corner by the desk, that this would, perhaps, be the last year this abandoned house could stand through the weather and still be considered adequate shelter. It was that thought of time passing that prompted him to consider making another trip to the plane. This time, with his strength about him, he thought he could look at the radio with much less despair.

Before he had a chance to suggest it to Walter, though, they went to sleep one night and awoke to the sound of laughing, irreverent voices and a flashlight, penetrating the darkness through the boards over the windows.

Walter bounced up like a toy on springs, and Nate, for all the aches of the day, was not much slower. The two of them grabbed their clothes and their sheets, and moved silently across the threadbare carpet, then tiptoed up the stairs.

"Our boots!" Walter's lips touched Nate's ear when he whispered, and Nate's body responded, heedless of time or place.

"Front porch," Nate whispered back, his nose buried in the curling hair over Walter's ear.

"On the ground, next to the steps," Walter said quietly. Oh hell—hopefully they wouldn't be seen in the dark, because there was no grabbing them now! Walter pulled ahead and Nate followed him up the stairs, left into what looked like a playroom, then to the left again into a large closet, then—

"Gracious." Mostly he mouthed the word. The back of the closet made a left turn into nowhere. Perhaps it had been meant to be a shoe rack, or a place for a cabinet that had never been built, but it disappeared, a slim crawl space, and Walter was shoving him backward into it.

Then shoving himself backward against Nate.

Nate pressed flush against the wall, knowing what Walter needed. A quick flashlight over this area would reveal what? A cabinet where none was? It was a tenuous place should anyone actually venture into the closet, but whoever was coming into the house—

Nate heard the front door pushed in, and the voices got louder. In fact, they were disturbingly loud, and he pushed his ear against the wall to listen.

"They're speaking French," he murmured, and Walter threw a heated glare over his shoulder. Nate grimaced and pressed his ear closer, listening in to what was, undoubtedly, courtship conversation.

"You're right: nobody is here," said a distinctly feminine voice. Nate had spoken school French and the French from the book he'd been reading Walter— Where was that? Oh, thank heavens, it was under the couch! This was . . . young French. Uneducated. The cant was distinctly working class, even Nate could hear it.

"Someone was here," laughed a young man. "See? Cards."

"What would Jews have to do with cards?" asked the girl.

"Nothing. But this wasn't discarded by the family. They all ran away before the war. This was left by squatters, like us."

"Ooh, think they'll show?"

"I hope not," muttered the young man. "I've got better things to do than play cards."

Nate heard a playful squeak next, followed by laughter, trilling, breathless, blatantly sexual.

And then *every* sound was blatantly sexual.

Nate let out a long, low breath, plastering himself against the wall even more as the young man's filthy laughter rumbled through the empty house. The young woman was brazen, begging for his tongue on her, complimenting the size of his cock. Nate grunted in discomfort at that, thinking about sex, a naked man, hearing his grunts and his moans, as clear as a bell rung in temple.

Walter's body fitted itself against his, heat emanating from his skin, through their clothes, the small of Walter's back even with Nate's swelling, aching groin.

Surprise and capture might have diminished the flood of Nate's lust, but they weren't being surprised and captured.

They were listening to sex, loud and wanton, and the tight, sturdy body Nate had yearned for was rubbing against his cock.

Nate dropped his head, burying his nose in Walter's neck, and groaned. Better Walter should hate him than they should be captured, he thought fuzzily. Walter *had* to be still, because it was both of their fates if he lost his mind.

He turned his head and nuzzled the hair at Nate's temple.

Then, oh God, he reached behind him, wedging his hand in at the small of his back, and grabbed Nate's cock.

Nate bit him, hard, in the juncture of neck and shoulder, the pleasure absolutely painful.

He heard Walter's gasp, but it was low, an almost invisible sound, especially in light of the squealing below them. He must have had her bent over the couch because they heard the furniture move with every thrust, and the young man's own sounds were not getting any quieter.

Walter squeezed him again.

Nate wrapped his arms around Walter's shoulders and hung on as a black wave of gilt fireworks exploded behind his eyes. Walter wiggled his hand, worming it under the waistband of Nate's drawers, and his bare skin against Nate's drew a sob against his will.

Walter turned his head and whispered, "Sh," briefly before catching Nate's mouth and squeezing and stroking some more.

Nate closed his eyes, tasting Walter—heat, the sweet rot of sleep, their attempts at keeping their teeth clean by using their fingers and baking soda from the medical kit. The sex going on downstairs continued loudly, unapologetically, but Nate's world began and ended in the awkward pressure of Walter's hand.

They were nearing a climax downstairs, and Walter stroked harder, faster, scooting forward just enough to give him some room. Nate clung to the kiss, to the intimacy of their mouths fused together, of the unspeakable, unbearable things Walter was doing to his body in the invisible closeness of this tiny den within a den.

Nate's climax rushed him, and he deepened the kiss until he was practically crawling inside Walter, and Walter jerked on his cock with as much movement as he could manage without venturing from their hiding place. Below them, the girl screamed, perhaps reveling in the abandoned house, and the boy grunted in what was probably climax.

And Nate geysered seed all over Walter's hand and backside, clinging to Walter and trying not to sob as his vision dimmed and his knees gave.

The house went quiet, the murmurs and laughter of the lovers subdued now that the act was over. Nate broke off the kiss with Walter, dropping his arms and keeping his face buried in Walter's curling red hair.

Walter shifted, pulling his arm from what must have been a cramped position behind his back and bringing his hand to his lips.

He grunted, softly, meaningfully, and Nate opened his eyes. They adjusted to the closet's darkness in time for him to watch Walter stick his tongue out deliberately and lick the webbing between his thumb and forefinger.

Equally deliberately, he popped his thumb into his mouth and sucked the smear of seed off it. And then his first finger. And then his second.

Nate watched him, breathless, mesmerized, his message absolutely explicit. There was no excusing this. Walter's hand behind him might have been help for a friend, or a way to keep Nate from giving away their position by holding his manhood hostage. It could have all been explained, or ignored, even the soul-melding kiss.

But not this. Not Walter, meeting his eyes in the dark, licking Nate's cum from his hand. Walter opened his mouth and gave his nose a little jerk. Nate lowered his head, his heart so thick in his throat that he wasn't sure he'd be able to answer with a spoken word.

"You," Walter rasped, lips touching Nate's ear. "Me. Bed."

Nate's breath caught in his throat, but he nodded, weak in spirit, apparently, because he didn't want to fight anymore. "Yes," he whispered. "Yes."

Downstairs, the lovers were murmuring, and then there was the unmistakable sound of the pump being primed. Once, twice, there we go, a gush of water, probably to clean them both off. Nate could sympathize.

Walter and Nate held their breath, listening to the quiet. Nate propped his back against the wall and made himself comfortable, wet shorts and all. After a pause, and a thought, he wrapped his arms around Walter's shoulders and pulled him to actually lean his slight weight on Nate's body. He closed his eyes then, hearing the comfortable postcoital murmurs, oddly tender after such an athletic-sounding bout of sex, and concentrating on the slack, easy weight of Walter against his body.

His breathing evened out, and Walter turned his head, resting it against Nate's shoulder. Nate rubbed his chin against Walter's hair, and Walter wiggled against him—not in a tantalizing way, but like he was burrowing, seeking shelter, seeking safety.

An emotion roared through Nate then that was so powerful that by the time Nate remembered his breathing again, he was surprised the house hadn't shaken, the woods hadn't rippled with the force of what ripped through his heart.

Nothing to do, nothing to do, but stand there in the darkness and hold Walter, hold him and count his breaths, and treasure his body, warm, sweating a little in the closeness of the closet, and wish.

The couple left near dawn, and by then, most of the thoughts of what he and Walter would do in bed had flown from Nate's head. He was exhausted and sore from standing in the cramped closet, and even the feeling of Walter's skin had begun to pall when they had been mashed together, without respite, for so long.

The front door slammed, and both of them startled from the semidoze they had fallen into, and Nate counted his own breaths to keep from bolting out of the closet, body screaming for space and air.

One . . . two . . . three . . . forty . . . fifty-five . . . ninety-eight . . . one hundred . . . one hundred twelve . . .

Walter took two steps forward, over the sheets and clothes they'd dropped as they'd crept into the hole, and caught himself on the wall when shaky legs threatened to give out. He turned and held his finger to his lips and gestured to the house.

Nate nodded. His wounded leg and his ribs were aching from standing so long. He would need to stretch and shake out his muscles if he were to run anywhere. He would love to be the one out there taking the risks, but Walter was better equipped to get away.

Walter ventured out, popping back after a moment, his arms full of sheets and his medic's bag dangling from his hand. Nate had propped his hands against the wall and was stretching his body, trying to work up the strength to move.

"They're gone. Here, help me make the bed, and we can get some shut-eye," he said, his voice abnormally loud in the quiet house.

Nate nodded and took the sheets from his hands, and Walter bent and picked up the things he'd brought with him from downstairs.

"They saw our boots," Nate said, his voice feeling rusty. "They must have."

"Well, maybe they saw them but didn't think on them," Walter replied practically. "They sort of had other things on their minds."

"Zol Gott mir helfen!" Nate swore—it had been one of his grandfather's favorites.

"That sounds like Jerry talk," Walter muttered, surprised.

"It means 'God help me,' because those two . . . they wouldn't leave, would they! They were going to go at it until we both dropped from exhaustion."

Walter's chuckle was subdued, tired, and as distraught as Nate felt, but it still felt good to hear. "I didn't even have to speak French to know she was saying, 'Do me, big daddy, like I ain't ever been done before!'"

Nate was too tired even to blush. "Lick up, down, to the left, faster, slower, right there—good. You might have it now."

Walter collapsed, leaning against the wall, dropping all the things in his arms in a silent convulsion of laughter. "She did not!" he managed between gasps.

"She did!" Nate protested. "I'm serious. Poor man! With a woman who gives directions like that, you'd have to be mad to want to make love to her."

"Yeah, well, it's not like you're expecting two guys in the closet, taking notes and making a . . ." Walter picked himself up off the wall and managed to shoulder his way into the main bedroom.

"Critique," Nate said, his voice sobering. "A critique. I don't imagine anybody likes a critique when making love." The bed loomed, red maple, stained nearly black and still shiny with lacquer under the dust. The mattress looked old, used well, stained, and a little flattened, but not soiled. Just . . . used.

"No," Walter said, and to Nate's relief, he drew a little nearer, bumped shoulders with Nate, and touched his arm briefly with his chin. "Nobody does."

Wordlessly, Nate spread a sheet on the bed and set about tucking in the military corners while Walter folded their clothes again and set them on the vast dresser that matched the bed. The two pieces were solid and well made but wouldn't travel well.

"They were Jewish," Nate said into the predawn quiet. "The people who owned this place. They fled before the Nazis got here."

"Good," Walter said, but like he was taking the observation seriously. "Nobody wants to be around when the Nazis are here, but it's worse if you're not blond and blue eyed." Conscientiously, he finished up with the clothes, then picked up more of the sheets they'd been sleeping on and used them as light covers on top of the bed. "It's colder in here away from the stove. I think there might be a blanket or two."

"That's a good idea," Nate said on a yawn. "I wish there were pillows."

Walter's only reply was the sound of rummaging and swearing. He came back with an armload of wool blankets—two of them decidedly moth eaten but also a large one that looked mostly untouched. Nate pulled one of the extra sheets off the top of the bed, suddenly excited.

"What are you doing?" Walter sounded cranky and out of sorts. And who wouldn't be?

"Rolling them together to make a bolster," Nate replied, using the bed as a table. Sure enough, with some rolls and some tucks, it would reach completely across the head of the bed.

Walter yawned and waited patiently for Nate before spreading the blankets and pulling back the sheet. The bolster was a little flat, spread out for two, but with some fluffing and some punching into shape it looked much more comfortable than the bolster on the arm of the couch or love seat, which had been giving them both headaches since Nate had first been brought here.

"Why did you do it?" Nate murmured, sliding under the sheets and feeling loopy with exhaustion. The windows up here were better boarded; this room would probably stay cool and dark well into late morning.

"Do what?" Walter slid in next to him, tucking something from the medical bag under his pillow as he did so. They rolled to face each other in the dim light.

"Go save me. It was such a brave thing to do."

"I was lonely," Walter slurred. "And God sent me you."

"It appears I was special made," Nate replied dryly, and to his relief, Walter smiled, even though his eyes were closed.

"Yeah, I think that's just proof that God loves poofs too."

Nate chuckled, and then one last thought overrode the pleasantness of falling into a deep sleep. "It was real, right?" he whispered, thinking Walter was asleep. "It happened."

"I held your cock in my hand," Walter confirmed, eyes still closed. But his lips were quirked up on the sides. "And you kissed me like it meant something. Don't worry, Nate. There's more reckoning to do."

"Thank heavens," Nate whispered, grateful as he'd never been grateful before. "It was wonderful."

Walter pulled Nate's hand toward him and kissed the soft-skinned knuckles. That was how they fell asleep.

RECKONING

W arm, masculine lips moved along his collarbone, and stubble rasped his neck. Nate *hmm*ed and stretched, trying to reconcile the sensation to the world as he'd known it. He'd never awakened with a lover in his bed, had never experienced lips on his bare skin, had only ever dreamed that the person—the *man*—he desired actually wanted him back.

There was a man in his bed. The man's hands were gliding on his chest, his stomach, his hip, and Nate grunted in surprise and want.

He opened his eyes and saw Walter, his red hair falling across his forehead and in front of his heart-shaped face, as he pointed his tongue and licked at Nate's nipple through his T-shirt.

The world stopped, and Nate took another one of those mind-pictures that he'd been filing away since his plane went down. Etched in his mind for eternity, a blue-eyed man, tangled red hair falling from being wet-combed and slicked back, a studious look crinkling the corners of his mouth and quirking up his lips, and that wicked pink tongue extended.

And the shutter clicked, and Nate's body became light and sound, soaring like a spitfire toward the precipice of instant arousal.

He gripped Walter's head, fingers clenching in that amazing hair, and bucked his hips, suddenly so hungry for Walter's body he wanted to shout with it.

Walter's chuckle vibrated under his fingers, and Walter tilted his head and licked his lips.

"You know what would be *amazing*?" he whispered.

"If you did that again?"

"If I did it when we were *naked.*"

Nate smiled shyly, suddenly more aware of his otherness than ever before. "Your body is so perfect."

He ran his big hand down Walter's back, along his backside, kneading a little at the scant padding of muscle there. He smiled, but then his father's face, the face of the rabbi at temple, his mother's disapproval, all snuck behind his lazily closed eyes for a moment. He snapped them open again and saw Walter, propped up on his chest hopefully, unaware that there had ever been a doubt, a fear, a hesitation in Nate's heart at all.

He was looking at Nate hungrily, naked yearning apparent in his eyes.

"I don't care about perfect," Walter said harshly. Nate moved his hand from Walter's backside to his cheek and cupped it fondly, the transparent stubble rasping his hand. "I want you so bad."

Nate palmed the back of his head and lifted up, pulling Walter into a kiss. Their teeth weren't brushed, but that was minor unpleasantness compared to wet, hungry open mouths fused together. Nate's virginity was lost in a haze of Walter's taste, his feel, even the earthy smell of him, particularly musky, pungently male.

Walter lunged upward, pinning Nate down against the makeshift pillow, storming his mouth like a conqueror, and Nate gave up willingly. His whole life of reserved, quiet people, yearning glances, perhaps the faint inkling that somebody, *somebody* might desire him back, and he'd never had this. *Never* had passion and want, so furiously undisguised.

Walter knew how to kiss, and he knew what he was doing. In no time, he'd straddled Nate's hips and was wrestling his shirt off. Nathan's hands were still tangled in the soft knit when Walter whipped his own shirt above his head. His knotty body, tight with muscle, narrow because they did not eat steak every day, was close, so close, and Nate was desperate to untangle himself.

"I want to touch you!" he panted, and Walter pulled back, his expression luminescent.

"That's wonderful. You keep right on wanting that. I'm *dying* to be touched!"

Nate freed his hands and slid them down Walter's ribs, shivering in the sensuality of skin on skin. Walter deepened the kiss and flattened himself against Nate so their bare chests were sliding together, and Nate did everything but wrap his legs around Walter's hips and trap him there in one big bare-bodied caress until he couldn't help himself from wanting . . . what?

What do you want, Nate? You know there's a name for it.

But there was no time. Walter was shaking, grinding his groin into Nate's and grunting softly. His body started to shake, and he dug his fingers into Nate's shoulders, and then groaned quietly into Nate's mouth and pushed down harder. His entire body went rigid, and he threw back his head, opening his mouth, squeezing his eyes shut. Nate wrapped his arms around Walter's shoulders even tighter, grounding him, keeping him from flying apart.

A spurt of hot wetness seeped through Nate's underwear, and Walter collapsed against him, panting. "I'm sorry. I'm sorry. I didn't mean to shoot so fast, but . . . God. I'm sorry. I needed that so bad!"

Nate bucked up against him, trying to say, *That's all right,* but his erection was weeping at the head, the glorious, shameful mess at his groin staying slick and hot. He made a noise of frustration, incompletion, and Walter chuffed laughter against his neck.

"I hear ya. Not fair to promise and leave you hanging." He kissed Nate's neck, scraping his teeth lightly, then dragged down to Nate's collarbone. His tongue came out to play, the combination of lips, tongue, and teeth was exquisite, and Nate's hips undulated against the mattress.

"Torturer," he muttered, and Walter laughed softly before sucking Nate's nipple into his mouth and toying with the end. Nate gasped and thrust a little more solidly against Walter's body. The vibrations of Walter's gentle, teasing laughter made Nate even crazier, and his hips rocked regularly. Walter's hand, bold as brass, thrust against the join of Nate's hip and leg.

"Nope. No getting off without me," he said firmly. "Hang on. I'm gonna make this good for you."

His hand down Nate's shorts was assertive, no-nonsense, and heavenly. And then he wiggled, the little touches of his skin and semen-soaked shorts tantalizing and unbearable. Nate rambled, strung-together gibberish mumbles. "Walter, what . . . Wait, I don't . . . No . . . *Yes!*"

The air hitting Nate's cock was almost painful, he was so aroused, and the heat of Walter's mouth was a detonation. His body soared, and the noises he made—*oy!* He would be embarrassed later, but in this moment, his entire being was shaking and his arms flailed, pounding the bed on either side of him. Walter kept up pressure and then started to stroke up and down. He used one hand to cup Nate's balls and to tickle the area behind them, to slide around in the spit and the pre-cum and tease. He used the other to push against Nate's chest as Nate tried to come off the bed.

Nate spread his legs and bent his knees, using the extra leverage to pump up hard, and Walter engulfed most of him, sucking intensely.

Nate's whole body shook cold, and his groin, stomach, perineum, asshole, clenched and exploded.

He let out a roar that rattled the wood in the window frames as he climaxed. Walter kept his mouth over Nate's cock and kept sucking, his throat working intensely while Nate spasmed beneath him. Finally, Nate pulled loose and rolled to his side, drawing his knees up and gulping air, his mind a stunned blank and his body a quivering, sensitive nerve.

He'd been beating off in the private dark since he was twelve years old and still what had just happened with Walter was a complete surprise.

The silence that settled over the darkened little room was filled with their harsh breathing and the sound of birds outside.

"What are you thinking?" Walter said behind him. Nate felt something hovering above his arm and realized that Walter had moved, and his hand was a finger's breadth away from caressing Nate's arm.

And that he was afraid.

"I'm thinking that was terrific," Nate said, feeling honest. Walter's hand settled on his arm, and some tension leaked out that Nate hadn't known he'd been holding. With a sigh, he let go of his surprise and the aftershocks that kept rippling all points south, and rolled back over. Walter looked worried, and Nate—no matter the ghosts of his father, his rabbi, and his mother that haunted behind his eyes—didn't want that.

He extended his arm and smiled faintly. Walter laid his head on Nate's shoulder, and they made themselves comfortable. Soon, the call of nature would need to be answered, and they would have to get food. Walter had kept drippings from the meat they'd cooked, and he'd been making a serviceable fried bread for the last few mornings. Once, he'd even found some quail eggs to add to it, and that had been delicious too.

"You've never done that before," Walter said frankly, but Nate was too satisfied to blush.

"You have," he said, carefully leaching any judgment from his voice. He was jealous; he could admit that in his own heart. What he felt for Walter was huge, all-inclusive. He'd done something with this man that he had never contemplated doing with another man—had, in fact, chosen unavailable men, men with girlfriends or wives to dream about, so that he would never have to choose between faith and desire.

There had been no choice here. Not since the closet had revealed him. Not since Walter had licked his hand and looked Nate nakedly in the eyes, proclaiming without words, *This, this is who we are. Cum eaters, cocksuckers, ass fuckers—you know this. We have no excuses.*

Nate wanted this to mean something to Walter too, but he was not sure how to ask.

Walter nodded, unashamed. "Yeah. Them Indian two-spirit kids—they were pretty good at this shit. I was white," he said apologetically. "I was good enough to fuck and all, but they didn't want to bring me into the tribe." Nate heard the sadness there, and his comforting pat on Walter's shoulder was automatic. Lonely. He'd been exiled from a group of his peers because of something he hadn't been able to control. Nate knew that feeling, even if his own exile had been self-imposed.

"I would have thought . . ." Nate hesitated to bring the name up. The talk of running around with other young people and simply *sharing* sex made Nate supremely uncomfortable. But it was not commitment. It was the sad *yentzen* of the ugly girl at the school dance, the one who could be had for a smile and a soda because she was sure that was the only love she would get, but it was not real love.

"Jimmy," Walter murmured, and the name alone made Nate's heart constrict. Jimmy, who Walter would have met in real life, who he would have seen in the drugstore or the grange. Jimmy could well be the love of Walter's life, and Nate just the poor replacement. Nate was very aware.

"You were very much in love."

Walter grunted. "Didn't think about it that way with Jimmy. He was just mine. He . . . he didn't start out a virgin, either, you know? We just . . . we checked each other out and knew—this person was safe." Walter's voice dropped. "I ain't felt safe my whole life. But me and Jimmy had each other's backs."

Nate was stroking Walter's arm absently, and when Walter shivered against Nate's chest, he tightened his hold. He had so many questions for Walter, but Walter wasn't going to volunteer any answers. Perhaps it was time for Nate to be brave. He had the officer's stripes—perhaps he needed to put himself in the line of fire.

"I have avoided this my entire life," he said baldly.

"Sex?"

Walter sounded so horrified, Nate had to laugh. "Loving someone so much I felt compelled to have it."

Walter made a hurt sound and rolled over to his side, propping up on Nate's bare chest. "You don't really mean that," he said and started to move off the bed.

Nate stopped him, holding his shoulders and making sure Walter could see his eyes. "You are the first man to look me in the eyes and say, 'We are like this,' and not apologize. To not make it dirty. I know we are trapped in this house, and we've been forced to be congenial to each other when we might ordinarily have just ignored the other's existence. But I couldn't ignore you now. I couldn't go back home and not hope to see you. If I saw you walking the street while I was on the way to temple, I would miss temple, grab you by the arm, and spend the entire day doing what we just did. I would never go to temple again."

Walter's forehead wrinkled, and his eyes grew shiny. "That's too many promises, and they're too big," he said, sounding upset. "I'm . . ." He breathed deeply and patted Nate on the shoulder. "I'm a *field worker*. I'm . . . If I hadn't signed up for the army, I'd be a hobo 'bout now. You can't . . . you can't go saying big things. Don't mean nothin' . . ." He turned his head away, wiped his face on the covers, then took another deep breath and looked at Nate with resolve. It was like he had a handle on what to do, what to say now. Well, good, because Nate didn't.

"You'll have a regular life after this, Nate. I'm something to toss away. I always have been."

Nate made an indeterminate sound—an angry sound—and grabbed Walter by the hair, pulling his head back. He lunged up, taking Walter's mouth, grinding into him, possessing him. Walter's arms flailed, beating against Nate's chest, and Nate kept the kiss, kept possessing, rolling over until he was on top, pressing Walter's slighter, stringier body into the mattress.

Nate felt the moment his resistance broke, and Walter quit struggling, went pliant, started kneading Nate's shoulders, burying his fingers in Nate's hair, begging for more touch.

Nate was the one who pulled back, and Walter lay beneath him, blue eyes huge, body limp and needy.

"I would not leave my faith for a man meant to be thrown away," Nate rasped and rolled off the bed and to his feet. He dressed, still angry, shoving his shirt over his shoulders and buttoning it with fingers made clumsy with emotion.

Walter, after lying on the bed wriggling and whimpering for a moment, made his way to his feet with shaky determination. He moved in front of Nate and grabbed his shirtfront, grumbling, "Here, let me." Competently, he started to button Nate's shirt. "Hell, I don't know if it's airmen or officers. You're always saying stop when it should be go and saying rest when we want to move. Saying love when it should just be fucking. And us enlisted men, we got no choice, you know?"

"You do," Nate said softly, taking his hands. They were shaking. "You could not enlist."

"I can't help enlisting," Walter said, voice bleak. "I was a goner from the first time that Indian kid winked at me and I sprung a boner. But . . . but I don't want that anymore. I don't want to be a plaything. I wouldn't mind being just a grunt, like with Jimmy. Having each other's backs. That was good. That hurt when he died. I won't lie. But you, Lieutenant Meyer . . . you're—" Like his hands, his voice was shaking, and the emotion Nate had hoped for was there for the hearing.

"Shh," he murmured, "*sha shtil*." He was not sure how he had come to be the leader here when Walter seemed to know so much more about being what they were. "It's fine, Walter. It's a—" he flailed for a metaphor "—a field promotion. You have gone from not very important to very important. I don't know how to fight the battle on the ground. You know that. But I know the big things. The important things. What battle we're fighting. Why we're doing it." His voice softened. "Why it's necessary."

Walter turned a vulnerable face to Nate then, and Nate's mind took another picture. Walter's eyes, red rimmed, his hair, greasy and falling forward into his eyes, and his lower lip, trembling and full.

"And why is it necessary?" he asked, and he craved something from Nate, something huge.

"Because people need to be needed," Nate said, trying to smile.

"I don't know about needing," Walter muttered, like he was trying to deny it. But he was naked, gazing up at Nate, and no pretense would veil his features, no matter how hard he tried. Eventually, he surrendered. "I wanted you so bad," he whispered.

Nate took his mouth softly, tasting salt. He pulled back and rubbed his thumb along Walter's lower lip.

"I wanted you too. But if I did not love you by the time we were in that closet, I would have moved your hand."

"You would not!" Walter argued, genuinely upset, it seemed.

Nate nodded, touching lips again. "I would," he said, meaning it. "There is much to love about you, Walter. I wish you saw it."

Walter turned away, looking for his own clothes. "That's a fancy boy's way of talking right there," he said, and he was trying to be practical, Nate could tell. "Men don't talk like that."

"Of course," Nate said with a sigh. "Because we wouldn't want to be queer or anything."

"I *am* queer," Walter snapped. "That don't make me not a man."

"Does being in love make you weak?" Nate asked, trying to follow Walter's train of thought. He was running up against something here, something as infuriating as the fact that Nate's family had more money or Nate had been to college, and Nate couldn't put words to it.

"Fucking's fucking," Walter snarled. "But love is for the rich. My dad married my mom 'cause she was knocked up. You can be in love, and people think that's just fine. If I'm in love, I'm a pansy. I'm in love with a *man*, and I might as well cut off my own balls, 'cause a man don't fuck for love. Not where I'm from."

Nate pulled on his trousers and buttoned them while Walter raged, and then stood for a moment without replying. His boots were downstairs, and suddenly that's where he wanted to be, whether or not his temper cooled enough to want to be with Walter again.

"We're both men, Walter," he said wearily from the doorway. "That's why we're both in this room."

"Where are you going?" He looked earnestly worried, and Nate kept that thought close to his chest.

"To the outhouse. I don't know about you, but it's past time I relieved myself."

"Oh." Walter's mouth opened and closed helplessly, and Nate took grim satisfaction in the fact that he didn't seem to have a response. Nate padded down the stairs with what dignity he had left.

CLOCKS

He didn't return to the house immediately after putting his boots on and using the outhouse. Instead, he went around the garage, to the back where the garden that had provided such bounty sat. He looked around, wondering what remained that Walter hadn't picked yet. He saw a patch of cattails by the irrigation ditch and walked there, pulling out the older ones to wash off the roots in the small stream.

He knelt in the rich black earth, feeling the sun on his back, and closed his eyes as the water sluiced over his hands. How long had Walter lived here, alone, during the winter months? What was it, early May? Nate's plane had gone down over a month ago, but Walter had been in this place in the depths of winter, living off canned preserves and caught game. His lover had been killed; he'd been captured, then escaped under brutal circumstances, and arrived here. Where he'd spent months when the woodland, the garden, and the house itself were covered in snow.

How long would Walter have to stay here? How long would he have to gaze through the boarded slats of the deserted house before his heart froze? Before he believed that love was an illusion, and that joy was for anyone, anyone besides the man who had never had another soul to cling to?

Nate had just reconciled himself to working a little harder, being a little more patient with his stubborn lover when a woman's voice sounded across the clearing.

"*Bonjour*!" she sang in French, and Nate shot to his feet and started running, stopping halfway to the house to drag in air because he wasn't quite ready for a sprint.

"No! No, don't go," she continued in that musical, lower-class French. "If I meant you harm, I would have told Horst about the boots!"

That froze Nate in his tracks. The boots—the boots he and Walter had placed outside the doorway. Slowly, he turned around and saw the girl to match the voice. Dark hair, dark eyes, tiny upturned nose, and a square jaw—unmistakably French. She emerged from the forest growth surrounding the garden clearing and regarded Nate cannily. He regarded her back, staying stubbornly silent. He was not sure his French was up to conversation.

"Yes, see? You are the one with the larger boots. Where is your smaller companion?"

Walter. "I am alone," he said shortly in French, hoping his accent was close to the working-class French this girl spoke.

"*Mesonge!*" she exclaimed, laughing. Lies. Bullshit. Well, it was, but she didn't need to know that.

"What is it you want?" he asked, not joining her in laughter.

"I thought you'd want to know," she said, arching her brows lazily over her brown eyes, "the man I'm fucking, he's an officer in the SS. At night, you should maybe tuck your boots in, or I'll have to tell him why I can't return."

Nate almost dropped his water. He had to knot his stomach to keep from disgracing himself right there as he stood at the edge of the irrigation ditch. When he spoke, his mouth was gummed together by sudden dryness and his voice crackled like dried leaves.

"That is good to know. How often do you plan to be fucking him in the abandoned house?" Their home. *Not a home. An abandoned house.* The first place he and Walter had made love. It was theirs. They had mourned the family who had left it, and now they would leave it too?

"He has a day off next week—same time, same place. I plan to be there at his leisure," she replied, nonchalantly, and Nate racked his brain for the words she was using. She was trying to tell him something.

"Will there be any other plans made for that night?" he asked, and she primped her hair with one hand. The action was unnecessary. It was in a sturdy braid down her back. She was wearing men's trousers, which fit tight around her hips, and a man's shirt. She looked at ease in these clothes, and they were frayed at the cuffs and at the knees. He thought perhaps she was more used to roaming these woods than he was. For his part, he was grateful that he'd been wearing some of the lighter summer clothes that Walter had found in the garage. They very nearly fit him—only a little loose in the legs and thighs—and they had no betraying insignia for military.

"*My* only plan is him," she said archly.

"Did anybody *else* have any plans?" he asked. The French Resistance. Hector had been helping OSS officers foster resistance near Provence Claire La Lune. *Oh God, father of serendipities, let there be a way to be lifted out of enemy territory.* That canister of film sat accusingly in the back of the cupboard, and Nate would dearly love to send that to Naval Intelligence to see what it contained. What hornet's nest had he stirred by taking recon pictures unexpectedly? What had been worth calling in untold numbers of planes and starting a major dogfight to protect?

The girl smiled insolently—and also as though she approved of the question. "Maybe you and Mr. Little Boots hide yourselves real good next week, and if nothing stops my plans, I'll come tell you about them."

Nate nodded. The food could not hold out forever. Eventually, he and Walter were going to have to try to venture into town. But here, it appeared, they had found an ally—perhaps.

"Next week," Nate said, wondering if he and Walter could spend the next week sleeping in the garage.

"*Oui,*" the girl said, cracking her gum. Abruptly, her expression sobered. "And I'd advise you to trust me on this," she said, meeting Nate's eyes. "Your accent is atrocious—American French always is. You can't go into town speaking that French, and there are posters about turning in Jews all over town. I don't care if you're Lutheran—with your looks, you'll find yourself in an SS Office, producing your pedigree. Unless your companion is a native, I suggest you hold tight in your little house and wait for me to get back to you. I may have a way to help you take a trip."

Nate nodded. "*Oui,*" he said, making sure his voice was measured. "*Il est toujours agréable de voyager en été.*" It is always agreeable to travel in the summer.

"It is indeed," she confirmed. "Especially with a charming companion."

"I have a charming companion," he told her, praying he wasn't betraying Walter in the worst of ways. "All I need is a destination."

She nodded. "We can give you that, my friend. Have faith. Next week. Same time. If you want me to see something, leave it in plain sight. Otherwise, hide everything—boots included—and make sure you and your companion can't be seen from a cursory inspection of the house. I should hate for *my* companion to get adventurous. It was all I could do to keep his attention away from your boots and your cards this time."

Nate grimaced. "You did a very good job of it," he said politely, remembering the way she had issued such explicit directions.

She had a lush mouth, painted red, and he could admit that if he leaned that way at all, he would have been watching her lips purse with undue fascination.

But now, he only waited to see what the woman would tell him.

"I'm glad you approved," she murmured. "I could boss you around a little, should you want it."

Nate flushed under the hot sun of the clearing.

"I am afraid my heart is otherwise engaged," he said simply, and she shrugged. He was flattered: she was a beautiful woman, and it seemed as though she'd been interested. Well, good for her.

"Another time," she said, that lush mouth impossibly smug. "Until next week." She executed a little bow and faded back into the forest, leaving Nate standing with a handful of cattail roots and a furious need to pee.

He used the outhouse first and then, when his hands were shaking less, took the cattails into the house. The smell of fried bread hit him, and he smiled sadly. He'd been looking forward to that.

Walter was standing at the stove, finishing up with the last dollop of bread in the grease. "You took a while," he said, then his face lit up. "Cattail roots? I ain't tried them! Is that what took so long?"

"Yes," Nate said, taking them to the sink to wash. "No. Something worse." He was acutely aware of Walter's apprehension, his fear and vulnerability, as he washed off the roots and broke the shoots down to where they started to be tender enough to eat. He turned around then and dried his hands before looking at Walter and getting ready to speak.

"What?" Walter asked. He'd taken the pan off the stove and was regarding Nate with alertness. *Not a child.* No. But vulnerable still.

"You do recall how we left our boots outside last night?"

All of the color rushed from Walter's face, leaving his freckles in greenish relief. "Oh God."

And Nate told him about the pretty woman in the woods.

"She knew we were there?" he asked when Nate was done. "But didn't tell her man? That's—"

"Frightening," Nate broke in bluntly. "She promises to return next week."

"How do we know she's going to wait that long? She could come tonight! Or tomorrow! She could bring the entire German army marching—"

"It's France—"

"It could be Times fucking Square!" Walter cried. "You just . . . you let me finish breakfast and brought in cattail roots like nothing was wrong?"

"What if they're waiting for us to leave, Walter?" Nate said, his hands shaking with the thought of all they didn't know. "What if the whole conversation was a trap so they could keep this house intact, safe for other refugees, a honey trap for unwary flies?"

"That's insane," Walter snapped, running his hands through his hair. "That's insane. If she'd wanted us, she had us. If her boyfriend really is SS, we would be dead by now. Or captured. She's—"

"Resistance?" Nate offered, afraid to hope. "She knew about Provence Claire La Lune."

"What in the hell is that?"

"The place of the clear moon," Nate translated. "It's . . . Before I ran the mission, a friend of mine was going on recon to listen. There are OSS officers here on the ground. They broadcast useful information to circling planes, and the contact in the planes gives them instructions back. Did you know that?"

Walter's mouth opened and closed again. When he spoke it was in bitter mimicry. "'I'm not really an officer, Walter. I'm just like you are, Walter.' *No*, Nate, I did *not* know that, and it would have been *spectacular* information to have!"

"Well, it wasn't relevant to crashing a plane and falling in love!" Nate yelled back.

"Would you stop *saying* that?" Walter demanded, his voice breaking. He pulled his hands through his unwashed hair, and Nate had a moment to wish him clean and dressed in clothes that fit, dapper and pretty, so he would know that Nate's world—where you could be in love—was for him too.

"Why?" Nate asked, lowering his own voice and regarding his lover with compassion. "Now, of all times, is the time for you to know I love you. When tomorrow is uncertain, and we may be on the run, or worse. Isn't this when you want to know that you're important to me? That I'll care for you if I can?"

Walter's mouth went weak, like he was trying to square up his jaw and keep his lips from quivering. He ran the back of his hand over it, and then again, before sagging back against the counter next to the stove.

"It was hard enough," he said, almost to himself. "It was hard enough when we had something like a home. I could pretend, you know? This whole month, I been pretending. I could take care of us, and we could be friends. And then . . . you . . ." Walter looked up at him in agony. "How come you had to want me back? I don't want to leave this place now. Part of me wants to run, rabbit for the hills, live in a cave until this war madness is over. But most of me wants . . ." Walter swallowed. "We didn't do everything. We just . . . we just got to where we could sleep in that bed!"

Nate's heart did a curious thing in his chest. It swelled, stopped his breath, and swept away his fear. "We . . . we shall compromise," he said after a moment. He took a step toward Walter, and another, grasping those battered, fine-boned, slightly greasy hands in his own. "We shall stay two days. Three. We shall . . . sleep," he said with a half smile, "in the day. Anyone watching us shall have nothing to see. At night, we shall take the flashlight and clean out the garage, make a safe hole where we can watch the house. Two days, three—if we don't run at the beginning, they won't think we'll run at the end. We can watch for a few nights from the garage. If she does what she says, brings the young man here for a tryst and then leaves, we can trust her the next day. If she comes with soldiers, thinking she has lulled us into security, we will be well hidden, and we can see what she is up to."

Walter grunted and clenched his hands—seemingly unwillingly—around Nate's fingers. "Why can't we just run?" he grumbled, and Nate thought maybe he was trying to run more from Nate, from his unyielding declarations of love, than from this tiny home that he had established in the heart of chaos.

"Because," Nate said, stroking the backs of Walter's knuckles with his thumbs until they relaxed, "somewhere nearby is an OSS transmitting station. We can call for pickup—if someone lands and takes us home, I can send my film in. It's important, I feel it. You can find your unit—"

"And what? Get shipped to another front?" Walter asked bitterly. To Nate's horror, he started to cry rolling, angry tears. "Is that what you want? To see me shipped out again? To fight— I can die like Jimmy, and this can all be a big mistake."

Nate had never struck another human being in his life. He was so surprised that he'd done so now, at this moment, with this person he claimed to love best in the world, that he simply stared at Walter, the crack of his hand against Walter's cheek still ringing in the air between them. A welt, red against the white, began to rise, even as Nate watched.

They stared at each other in horror.

"Why did you do that?" Walter asked, sounding stunned, as well he might.

"You hurt me," Nate whispered, the red bloom in his chest raw and aching. "You hurt me. I had to make you stop."

"I don't under—" Walter raised his hand to his cheek.

"I don't want you to die, Walter," Nate said bitterly, turning away and staring out the one window in the house not covered with boards. "Can we just leave it at that?"

"Then what—"

"This war is terrible," Nate murmured. "It is terrible. There are things happening to Jews and Gypsies and . . . and *everybody* that I am afraid to think about. The rumors are bad enough. What if the rumors are true?"

"I don't—"

Nate cut him off again, turning to meet his eyes, to see the confusion, the bruise on his face, both things that he had done. "I am not thinking about the war here," he said bleakly. "Looking at you, I am thinking about after the war. I am thinking about how we would make a life together, somewhere quiet. How I would learn to live away from Manhattan and you would learn to live away from whatever hole in Iowa treated you with shame. The world would think we were friends. Bachelors who never married—there are many of them. I know a pair—and nobody thinks, 'Oh yes, they are lovers, married like a man and a woman,' but now that I've touched you, I'm pretty sure that is *exactly* what they are. And we could be them." A magpie landed on the bush outside and fluttered his wings with due arrogance. Would there be a flock nearby? Would they devour the garden or seed it? Nate didn't know about such things, but he could hope for the best.

"We could be what?" Walter's voice trembled with hope, and Nate allowed himself to think of him beyond the shame—both the shame for what he'd done to Walter, and the shame for what they'd done together.

"Together," Nate said softly. "Don't you want to be together?"

Walter closed his eyes. "It's a pretty idea," he said. "Nothing I can believe in, but it's pretty."

"Can you believe in it enough to stay?" Nate asked, closing his eyes and aching. "To stay and hope? To take a chance on tonight and tomorrow, and see if together we can imagine a time without a war?"

Walter's hand on his cheek was enough to make him open his eyes.

"I can't imagine that," he said frankly. "My whole life is some sort of war. But—" he grimaced, rolled his eyes, made light of it as though it were nothing "—I can take a chance on tonight. I can take a chance on tomorrow night. I think I'd risk about anything to see what could happen in that room upstairs, with a bed and you."

Nate smiled and kissed his palm. "Food first," he said soberly. "It is growing toward afternoon. Food first."

Walter nodded. "That fried bread ain't getting any fresher."

Breakfast was a little greasy but tasty, and they chopped the greens up and put them in the oven with the rabbit Walter had caught the night before, a century ago, before their safe little haven had been invaded. Afterward, they cleaned up, careful to put dishes in cupboards and remove all traces of themselves, stowing everything from the books to the playing cards in a slit of fabric behind the couch.

Walter decided to risk splicing some plywood into the closet, thinking that the wood there would make the alcove disappear even more effectively than the shadows. Nate told him to pull up some of the floorboards while he was at it and see if there was any way they could hide under the slightly higher end of the house.

The space was small, and Walter in a taciturn mood, so Nate concentrated on eradicating their presence, at least from the downstairs. The upstairs had two bedrooms, the main one where they'd slept the night before, and a secondary one with empty library shelves and a dresser. Nate chased out some spiders and a couple of field mice, and used the dresser to stow their clothes. There was a mattress in this room too, but the spaces between the wooden boards over the broken windows were bigger, so the water damage from the winter was worse. It smelled of mildew, and Nate was pretty sure there were creatures in the mattress that he hadn't had the honor of meeting in the main bedroom.

The last thing he stowed was the automatic pistol he'd had holstered when the plane went down. He'd cleaned and oiled it twice since he'd recovered, and had even worn it tucked into the waistband of his pants the other day when they'd walked to the plane. If he was going to sleep in the upstairs, cut off from the exit, the food, even the playing cards, he at least wanted his .45 nearby.

While Nate was stowing gear, he put two big cook pots full of water on the wood stove to heat. They weren't quite boiling by the time he was done hiding his and Walter's presence in the house as completely as he could, so he left the pots to heat and tromped up the stairs to root around the magic cupboard where Walter had gotten all of the linens.

There were still a few linens left but no toiletries, so Nate tried the washroom. He sighed once he saw it—delicate blue tiles, a toilet, a claw-footed iron tub. Oh, if only Walter had found the water main and the boiler.

Nate stared at it, though, thinking, and found the rubber plug hanging over the faucet and plugged it in. It seemed like it would hold. Then he rummaged under the cupboard, scaring some spiders down there and wishing heartily for a broom. It was worth it. A small glass bottle of bath salts lurked in the corner, unbothered by the webs. Nate fished it out and set it on the back of the toilet, and then began the arduous task of filling the bathtub with water. He was on his third trip with a bucket when Walter looked up from the game of solitaire he'd initiated after he'd finished his task in the closet.

"What are you doing?" he asked suspiciously.

"Filling the bathtub."

"But the water's got to be freezing!"

Nate nodded—some of that freezing water had sloshed down his leg. "Yes, but once it's sat out in the tub for a while, it will be warmer, and easier to heat with the water boiling on the stove."

"What's wrong with a navy bath?" Walter queried, eyes narrowed.

"Were you or were you not the one who yearned for a shower?" Nate asked shortly. "It was wise not finding the water main or the boiler. It's been risky enough just using the cook stove. We were lucky we hadn't started the fire in two days, or we'd probably be dead. But since we have one going now, I have an idea."

He wanted to see Walter's hair, bright and orange, like he'd seen it sometimes after the sponge baths, when he'd scrubbed particularly hard. He wanted Walter to feel healed and reborn, the dirt of his battle, his time as a medic, his escape, to be washed away.

He wanted Walter to feel clean and perfect, the way Nate had started to see him in the past month.

And Nate wouldn't mind feeling the same way.

He continued his trek, feet creaking on the boards of the house from the kitchen and the pump to the bathroom, shoulders aching but healed lung mostly sound. By the time the tub was half-full, long shadows stretched across the boarded windows, and the front window that opened for the pump was completely shaded. The water in the pots was almost boiling, and by the smell of it, dinner was close to done. Nate checked the rabbit and pulled the pan out, setting it on the counter.

"Walter," Nate said, moved by impulse. Two nights—isn't that what they had given themselves? Two nights to continue to play pretend?

"What?"

"Come here. If we sit on the porch, we can look to the west and see the sun set."

There was a stillness then, and Nate peered over his shoulder. Walter was shuffling the cards carefully before he set down the deck.

"Yeah," he said, his voice small. "Okay. That's . . . that's a nice idea."

The concrete stairway was narrow, so Nate sat on the top step and Walter sat on the step below him, between his splayed knees. The sun was only a few degrees over the horizon when they sat down, and Walter rested his elbows on Nate's thighs.

Nate leaned forward and put his hands on Walter's shoulders and his chin on the top of his head.

Together they watched as the sky turned the spangled gold of a burnished peach and threw the green and brown of the forest around them into stark purple relief.

"This is nice," Walter conceded, his voice hushed and reverent. "You got this in Manhattan?"

"Not like this," Nate said appreciatively. "But the brownstones, as the sun sets, loom like people with eyes. The happy houses seem to smile, the stern ones look forbidding. You can imagine them, *klatching* and *kvetching* at each other, sharing the news like yentas. In the evening, after traffic calms down in the summer, boys will play stickball in the alleyway, scattering like fish when cars turn down that way."

"Did you do that?" Walter asked, his voice curious as a child's.

"No," Nate said, at peace with who he was. "I did not. After my brother died, I was solitary, you know? My father . . . well, he loved Zev better. It was really that clear. And at first, I was always trying to be the good boy. And then high school arrived, and children were going to their bar and bat mitzvahs and planning who they would marry and . . ." He kissed the top of Walter's head. "It was clear to me at least, that was not the life I would have."

"What did you do?" Walter was as avid as he'd been when Nate was reading an adventure story.

Nate laughed softly, the sound blending seamlessly into the quiet noises of the woods. The cooling air smelled of pine and warm grasses, and of the lake, which he still had not visited.

"I became a *superlative* student," he said truthfully. "And I studied photography and took pictures of all the athletes, male and female, and nobody knew I liked the men better. So when I signed up for the air force, I was easy pickings for the OSS—exactly who they liked."

"Poofy as a queen," Walter chuckled, and Nate didn't take offense.

"As are you," he said mildly.

"Yeah." Walter closed his eyes. "It'd be so much easier if I'd never seen that Indian kid wink, you know?"

Nate kissed the back of his ear. "Something else would have done it," he said softly. "You would have enlisted, and Jimmy would have found you, or worse, you would have gotten sweet on an officer when you *weren't* stranded in a cabin in the woods like survivors on a desert island."

Walter tilted his face up to the last rays of the dying sun. "Have you ever heard church bells, Nate?"

Nate grunted. "Yes, sometimes. They are supposed to chime in Times Square for New Year's Eve, you know, as long as the war lasts. Why?"

"They used to ring through our town, every Sunday. My folks didn't go, but the sound . . . It was beautiful, right?"

"Yes. I think they all chime that way."

"See, that's what God's voice was to me. When I was a kid, I thought God's voice was the church bells, because the preacher said God was supposed to speak to everyone. And you know, everybody could hear them."

"Yes," Nate said, amused. "Even the Jews."

Walter turned in Nate's loose embrace, putting their faces close together. "That's what I'm talking about," he said earnestly. "It was like God was calling *all* of us. The Jews, the white kids, the black kids who went to the church with no bell. The Indian kids, even the two-spirit ones. I *believed* that, you know? And then I smiled at an Indian kid and my daddy blackened my eye, and it was like . . . like the whole world was one big lie, because God didn't talk to us all."

Nate closed his eyes then and simply breathed Walter in, the ugly and pure of him. Mostly the pure.

"That is an amazing thought," he whispered, moved in ways he couldn't voice. "Maybe that's what the bells at Times Square are for, on New Year's Eve."

"To call all of us," Walter said, his voice burning with that surprising idealism. Who knew? All of the cynicism, all of the doubt—all of it had been armor to the most tender of hearts.

"Yes." Nate's breath was harsh in his ears, and his eyes burned. "So if we get separated during the war, that is where we will meet, yes?"

"Times Square on New Year's Eve," Walter murmured, and Nate could feel the smile against his lips. "We'll meet at Times Square, whether or not there's bells, right?"

"Of course," Nate whispered. "That is where we'll meet. God will call us home."

Their kiss was warm and almost chaste, the seal of a vow, and Walter kept kissing, didn't seem to want to break it off. Finally, Nate pulled back, mindful of the water boiling on the stove, and when he opened his eyes, purple shadows had slid over the clearing, engulfing the forest. And straight above them, beyond the tips of the pine trees, stars like glass shards threatened to rain blood down upon their heads.

After dinner, he made Walter undress and put his clothes in the bathroom sink to soak, while he took the pots of boiling water upstairs. They had other clothes; Nate was not worried about the laundry. They put another two pots of water on the stove, warming them with the last of the wood for the day, and then Nate shooed Walter upstairs, naked, to the tub.

He'd poured some bath salts in with the hot water, and the result was fragrant, like roses. He held out his hand and helped Walter step into the tub. Walter winced at the heat, before Nate had him lie back.

"Here," Nate said, as Walter's muscles relaxed one at a time. "Let me soap your hair." He did, using the softened bath salts to work up a lather. Walter moaned in appreciation, and again when Nate soaped his chest and his upper thighs. His legs splayed open, leaving his privates vulnerable and bare, and Nate took special care soaping those too.

"Here," Walter said, opening his eyes. "Give me the cloth."

"What are you going to do?"

"Get my backside real good." Walter closed his eyes and pushed behind himself, grunting as he apparently scrubbed between his buttocks.

Nate's throat closed with the force of his arousal.

"I'm . . ." He was going to say, *Not sure we'll be doing the* mishkav zakhar, *my people forbid it*, but Walter's head tilted back, and his cock, long and slender, began to swell, the foreskin stretching to expose the perfectly shaped head.

And sweat started at Nate's collar and trickled down his chest and his underarms. Suddenly, he wanted that thing, the thing Walter was preparing for—the *mishkav zakhar*, the most forbidden way to spill seed that was not in a woman's womb; Nate was swollen and greedy for it.

He wanted to be inside Walter, driving away all doubt, wrapped up in his flesh. Walter was making himself clean for it, and Nate was hungry to take that offering.

He must have made a noise because Walter's eyes half opened. "I should get out," he said roughly, undulating his hips, thrusting his cock clear of the surface. "You deserve some warm water too."

Nate reached out with one finger and stroked that marble cock from the slick end to the hairy base. Walter's groin hair was a pale ginger, and Nate liked looking at it.

"You are beautiful," he said softly and then watched the flush blotch Walter's chest, not all of it from the hot water.

"Yeah, well, you too. Get naked. I wanna see."

Nate smiled shyly and began to strip while Walter stood, dripping into the tub. Nate draped his clothes on the bathroom vanity, dry as a bone, and then stood with the towel, waiting to help Walter out.

"I'm not a girl," Walter said, taking his hand. "You don't have to treat me like a princess."

Nate wrapped him up and pulled him back against his own nudity. The towel chafed pleasantly, and Walter's clean skin sent shivers down his spine.

"You're a prince among men," he murmured, letting his lips trail along Walter's neck. Walter's whole body rippled against him.

"You're full of bullshit and sunshine," Walter protested but without heat. "But I'll take it, just . . . Ah . . ."

Nate insinuated his hand under the towel and stroked Walter's pale stomach, his abdomen like a washboard and that lovely ginger hair growing sparsely below the navel.

"I'm going to get in the tub now," Nate informed him, making sure his breath hit the whorls of Walter's ear.

"Killing me," Walter whispered. "You're killing me, Nate—"

"I want you to see heaven tonight," Nate interrupted. "I want you to see it with me."

Walter leaned his head against Nate's shoulder and said nothing. It was enough.

The water was cooler when Nate got in, and the water downstairs was probably not close to boiling, so his bath was more matter-of-fact and less sensual. He let Walter soap his hair, though, and rinse it off, shielding Nate's eyes with his hand as he dumped water from a glass jelly jar.

"You have thick hair and a big head," Walter said, not sounding put out. "You look like you should be on a battlefield somewhere, you know? One of them Greek men, with a sword and a shield." Walter's hands stilled, and his next words were dreamy. "No one'd know you're about as fierce as an oak tree."

"That's an interesting comparison," Nate acknowledged, his eyes sill closed. "An oak tree?"

"Strong," Walter murmured. "Not violent. Unruffled."

Nate laughed, then cleared his eyes with his hands and sat up. "Loud," he said, smiling. "At least at first."

Walter shook his head and rocked back on his heels, the towel tied around his waist. "You warned me. You did. You said you were usually more reserved. And sure enough, the minute you recovered, you were closed like a clam."

"Yes, well, you're the only person to see me any way but that," Nate told him. With a heave, he stood up from the water and allowed it to sluice off him. "For a brief, shining moment, I was interesting, at the very least."

"Didn't say you weren't *interesting*," Walter corrected. "Just said you weren't *loud*. Would have made it easier if you'd stayed loud, because then I'd have known where we stood. You got all quiet and moony-eyed on me, and I was suddenly worried you didn't like me too."

Nate remembered the sulks and the way Walter had started calling him "sir." There was more to it than that, he knew, but yes, Nate's reticence had been part of it.

Walter checked his face in the resulting silence. "You're still funny when you're not loud," he reassured. "Don't ever forget that."

Nate shook his head, scattering water everywhere, and Walter laughed and hollered, "Not funny *that* way!"

"Then stop talking about my defects as a companion and get me the other towel," Nate complained good-naturedly, and Walter did so, grinning.

"I take it all back about being an oak tree. You're a big, happy dog, that's what you are. Easy to be around, useful when you're needed, and you can make a helluva mess."

Nate toweled off his hair roughly and then his chest. Walter had brought up their solitary comb from Nate's flight kit, and his hair was slicked behind his ears, the curls all scraped to the back of his head. Nate did the same thing, but his own curls were springier, erupting over his head in tight ringlets. He looked at his reflection in the mirror and sighed.

"If I'm lucky, it will fall out when I'm thirty. All of the unattractiveness, none of the upkeep."

"Shut up!" Walter slugged him in the arm like a schoolboy, and Nate grinned at him, knowing that the space in his front teeth was apparent.

"You wouldn't want to be seen with a bald man?"

"You're real handsome," Walter said loyally. "You're . . . you're *royal*, like someone important. I like it."

Nate's grin softened. "Good," he said simply. "I like that you like it. I would like to see the two of us in a picture, dressed in our best suits."

Walter's smile went dreamy. "Could I have a fedora? Those are . . . They're like what a gentleman would wear. I'd like that."

Nate could picture Walter in a snap-brim newsboy's hat for his youth, but yes. As an adult, as a *gentleman*, he'd get a fedora. "Of course," he said. It was his fantasy; Walter could wear a fedora and a tie. "Your tie must be of green silk," Nate told him. "And your suit can be dark gold."

Walter turned his head away, shy. "That sounds nice," he said. "In London, they've got bars—Jimmy and I went, when we were on leave before we shipped out. The guys dance."

Nate wrapped his towel around his hips and pulled Walter to his body. All those years at school dances, escorting the daughters of his mother's friends, and finally, *finally*, he got to dance with someone whose body he yearned for against his.

"Hmm, hmm-hmm," he sang playfully, and Walter tilted his head back and laughed. But he kept dancing.

"What are you supposed to be singing?"

"'A String of Pearls,'" Nate replied, wiggling his hips. "Lots of trombone," and bump and grind.

Walter relaxed into it and started singing with him. "Bump-a-dum-dun, dun, dun-dun!" Nate executed a little twirl in the dim confines of the washroom. They finished the song together and stood, breathless, looking at each other.

"What does the band play next?" Walter asked.

Nate lowered his head, so they were very close, and breathed his next words softly in Walter's ear. "'I'm Getting Sentimental Over You.'"

Walter laughed and rested his head against Nate's shoulder, and they danced to that one too.

When Nate had remembered as many words as possible, their feet stilled, and they stood in the closeness of the abandoned house, sweating slightly, skin pressed together, separated only by two thin bathing sheets that had seen better days.

"What would we do then?" Walter's eyes were big, limpid as lakes, and he looked amazed, in wonder at the moving lights and the sweetness of the orchestra, all of which were playing in their own minds.

"I'd kiss you," Nate said. He let go of Walter's hand and hip, and raked his fingers through that clean, burnished hair, and stood, their lips close together, sharing breath in the encroaching darkness.

"Then do it," Walter said. "I need that—"

His mouth was warm, wet, and responsive. Nate tasted and then fell, devoured, encircled by the haven of Walter's body, and Walter pulled him into the kiss unmercifully.

Walter broke off, took two steps for the hallway, and grasped the towel around Nate's waist, urging him forward into another kiss. Nate cupped the sides of his neck now, his thumbs stroking along Walter's jaw.

And pulled him in again.

And again and again. They kissed and stumbled down the hallway toward the bedroom, palms and fingers glutting on the delicious bare skin. Walter's shoulders were a little rougher, some of the freckles raised from the sun, but his shoulder blades beneath were as satiny as Nate had imagined. When Nate splayed his thumb and forefinger at Walter's throat, he could feel the rabbit pulse of Walter's heart against his palm, and every harsh breath echoed like a hymn.

For his part, Walter placed biting, nipping kisses around Nate's chest, across his collarbone, down to his dark, plum-colored nipple.

Nate tripped when Walter gave a hard suck, scraping the end between tongue and teeth.

"*God*!" He knotted his fingers in Walter's hair, not sure whether to pull him away or push him closer, but Walter was too wily to be trapped there for any reason. He extended his pointed tongue and swiped, slowly, to Nate's other nipple, and this one he suckled *and* licked, long drugging strokes, up and down, the pressure of his lips maddening, while Nate massaged the hard curve of his scalp.

"Walter . . . God, it feels so—"

Walter leaned back, releasing the nipple with a *pop*, and then lunged upward, taking Nate's mouth again, walking them backward until Walter bumped up against the bed and stopped.

He fumbled, first with Nate's towel and then with his own. They stood for a moment, hands rough on each other's cheeks, and Nate kissed him, teeth nibbling at lips, nose bumping along Walter's jaw, aggressive and needy.

Walter gave back, nipping, suckling, their cocks inflated and gliding together. Nate's ridge would catch on Walter's, the contact gentle and rough and exquisite, Walter's pubic hair a rasp against Nate's dripping head.

Walter broke the kiss, resting his forehead against Nate's collarbone. "I want your mouth on me . . . Can you do that?"

"Please," Nate begged, and without ceremony sank to his knees on the bare boards of the floor.

Walter's penis was lovely, straight and flushed rosy with desire. Nate licked experimentally, pulling back on the shaft and exposing the head. Walter's fingers massaged Nate's scalp through his hair, and Nate licked again, tasting salt, and again, tasting more. Encouraged, he opened his mouth and sucked Walter's flesh inside, keeping his hand wrapped firmly around the shaft.

Oh, Walter, your skin is so soft. But his shaft was rigid, and Walter's hips jerked as he tried valiantly not to drive his cock down Nate's throat.

Nate stroked his hand back and thrust his head down as far as he could go, gagging slightly on the liquid dripping against the back of his palate, and moved back to swallow.

"Good," Walter groaned. "So good. Do it again, Nate. Do it ag—" —ain.

And again. And again.

Nate's own arousal throbbed between his legs, bobbing against his hairy thigh, smacking with each movement, but that was secondary to the taste, the texture, of Walter's cock down his throat. He wanted more, *craved* more, and Walter wasn't holding back. Groaning, he thrust hard, hips and thighs vibrating as he drove himself forward and back, giving Nate just enough time to swirl his tongue around the head before driving down for another swallow.

"I'm gonna come!" Walter cried out, and Nate didn't know it was a warning until he convulsed, shoved his cock far into the back of Nate's throat and shot semen, in thick clots, against Nate's tongue.

Nate craved that too. He tried to swallow as Walter had, but the bitterness undid him, and he lost some around his mouth, down his chin. Still, he kept his mouth closed tightly, so Walter could spend himself completely. Nate wanted time, damn it. Let Walter come now; Nate was going to take him again, slowly, make him beg.

He wanted to be needed in the worst of ways.

Walter gasped, maybe Nate's name, and then his knees gave and he sat down on the bed, hands knotted in Nate's hair. He tugged, and Nate tilted his head back, unapologetic, only at the last moment swiping some of Walter's seed from his chin with the back of his hand.

Walter cupped his cheek and wiped the corner of his mouth with a rough thumb. "You're good at that," he panted, closing his eyes. With his flushed face and parted lips, he looked like an angel, and then he smiled with one corner of his mouth, and he looked decidedly unangelic.

"It was my first time," Nate said, licking around his mouth and preening. "I think I have a passion for the task."

Walter laughed, the sound edgy and hysterical. "That's funny right there. *That's* the guy who cracked wise while he was half-dead. And now you're gonna—um—"

Nate pushed up and kissed him, salt-bitterness and all, and Walter licked at his mouth hungrily. His hands bit into Nate's shoulders, and he clung, still needy, still desperate, and Nate tried to eat him alive, devour him, suck his energy and his verve and his solid, grounded little body inside so Nate could be that alive.

Walter pulled away, and Nate sought his mouth again, dazed.

"Gimme a minute," Walter half sobbed. "God, Nate. Gimme a minute. Need some grease, 'cause I need it. Need it bad."

"What?"

Nate blinked his eyes hard, hoping to clear the passion from them, and saw Walter fumbling behind him, under their makeshift pillow. He came back with a little tube of surgical gel, and Nate widened his eyes.

"What is that?"

Walter squirted a dollop on his hand and shivered. "It's cold," he said and then destroyed Nate, leveled him, detonated lust and abandon in his stomach and his chest, when he reached behind himself and lifted a knee off the bed so Nate could see him pushing the gel into his sphincter, shuddering with the cold and the feeling as he did so. "Ahh . . . *God*! It's so good, Nate. You gonna make it better?"

Nate sat up on his knees on the bed and reached for Walter's palm, warm and moist. He took some of the excess gel pooling in his palm while Walter's fingers were inside of him, scissoring, stretching, *pleasuring*. His own hand was shaking as he spread the gel on his dripping cock until Walter's hand joined it, lubricating and stroking at the same time. Nate closed his eyes and gasped, trying to get hold of himself before he came.

He thought about white semen shooting across the short distance to paint Walter's face and almost came anyway.

Walter squeezed his base, and Nate forced himself to meet his eyes.

"I need this," Walter confessed roughly. "I need *you*. You'll like it, Nate," he said, pleading. "You just stick it in, and it'll feel so good." He rocked onto his back, hooking his thighs with his hands and spreading himself for Nate to see.

Lewd, obscene, his swelling cock stretched across his stomach and his balls sagged toward his perineum.

His pucker, loose, dilated just enough to let Nate not fear to break it, gaped at him.

Nate leaned forward, kissed a stringy thigh covered with blond hair, and kissed up to the side of the knee. Walter made a strangled, keening noise.

"Take me," he begged. "Please. We only got so much time."

The world, caught for a moment in a jittery, greedy slice of frozen time just for Walter, suddenly started up again, steady as a ticking clock. "Yes," he murmured. Carefully, he placed the head of his cock—oh, it had never looked so big, so painfully swollen, as it did when poised to breach Walter's entrance—and prepared to push.

Walter made a frantic sound and humped down on the bed, begging, obviously wanting Nate's cock inside of him more than he wanted dignity or room to breathe.

Nate closed his eyes and thrust, letting Walter's yelp of pleasure/pain wash through him.

"*Yes. More!*"

Nate's eyes snapped open, and he took in Walter, head back, mouth open, eyes closed, wanton and lovely, and pushed forward some more. Walter wanted this, *craved* it, and his erect cock, leaking pre-cum again, was a testament to his hedonism, to the pleasure he took, and that was enough for Nate.

Walter's asshole squeezed Nate's cock in an embrace of moist heat and almost violent pressure.

Nate had no choice but to surge in, allowing himself to be stroked outside as he stroked Walter from within. When he was as far inside as he could be, he stilled, the slickness and the pressure so great, he shook, sweat tracking from under his hair down the side of his face. He closed his eyes, not wanting to move. It was perfect here. Beautiful. Everywhere he'd wanted to be, everything he'd ever thought about joining two people was here, in this one terribly forbidden act.

"Nate," Walter breathed. "Please. Please, don't just— You can't just . . . God, Nate, I need you to . . . Please . . ." He was gibbering, and Nate opened his eyes to hear this self-sufficient man plead for him, Nathan Selig Meyer, who was not a Greek warrior on the battlefield or a shining Aryan lion. Just him. The quiet boy, the loner, and Walter needed *him*.

"*Yes*," Nate hissed, pulling back and thrusting forward. His voice shook, his *body* shook, and he had no choice about seeking Walter's core again. He grabbed Walter's thighs and hauled him forward, resting his calves across his chest, and thrust hard, desperately, while Walter fisted the sheets, twisting them in his fury.

He moaned and pleaded breathlessly, and Nathan could do nothing for him, nothing but piston into him, *fucking*—a word that made his loins boil over with what it meant to be inside another human being.

Walter's cock flopped on his stomach, making its own slapping counterpoint to Nate's frenzied thrusting. With a heave, Walter flattened his thighs against his chest, and Nate fell forward, catching his weight on his elbows. Walter was helpless to move, caught under Nate's body, and Nate forced him to endure kisses, needy ones, on his face, on each eye, the end of his turned-up nose, the corner of his mouth. He kept moving, kept *fucking*, and Walter tilted his head back, baring his throat and moaning in guttural bursts.

He sounded feral, like a lynx or cougar, something that would hunt Nate and draw blood if he didn't give him what he needed.

"Look at me," Nate gasped. He was still short-winded; he would have to either climax or collapse. "Look at me, *tateleh*, do you see?"

Walter's blue eyes opened reluctantly. "I see you," he panted. "I see you. C'mon, Nate, let me . . ."

Nate propped up, adjusted his angle, kept throwing his hips but not as hard, not as furious, slower, deeper, and the ripple that rocked Walter's body was a glorious thing.

Walter let one of his legs go and grabbed his cock with a desperate fist. Nate wanted to watch him, doing another forbidden thing, brazen and screaming, but his orgasm, like a surging hurricane or an epic wave, was charging his perineum, his sphincter, his balls, his stomach, his chest, his . . . *oh God, my cock!*

He came, deep inside Walter's body, and Walter kept working himself with the brutal slap of his fist against his balls as he stroked his own erection.

Nate's vision blacked. For a moment, he was truly afraid, because his breath panted in short bursts, and his chest ached, and Walter's body had clenched him, like a finger trap from a joke store: the more Nate pulled, the harder Walter squeezed.

Then Walter gave a small cry, a keen, and his semen erupted, blowing in spatters across his tight stomach, his narrow chest. His sphincter relaxed, and Nate pulled out, collapsing to his side, head on his outstretched arm.

For a moment, the roar of their breathing was louder than guns, louder than airplane noise. For that moment, he was completely alone, and very much afraid.

What have I done? This thing, this one taboo thing, for which there is no forgiveness, no way to atone. And for a man who does not love me back.

Walter turned to him, blue eyes bright in the dark. He wiped his hand on the sheets and brought it up shakily to brush Nate's cheek.

"I hope there's no Nazis outside," he said frankly. "You were loud."

Nate smiled faintly, heart troubled. His body was assaulted by the most terrible languor, and he was truly afraid they would not be able to start their appointed task in the garage now that the dark had fallen fully.

"You are the only person in the world who would say that about me," he said.

Walter nodded, eyes searching his. "So that's a part of you I have," he said, his eyes starting to focus, moving cannily in the darkness. "I know you, that you're loud, and that you're funny. I know that you growl like a bear when you're inside me. I know that your cock has a flat spot, right under the piss-slit. Nobody else knows this, right?"

Nate's heart lost some of its trouble. "Only you," he said sincerely. "Come here, Walter. I'm lost and a little lonely. I don't know... I don't know how my heart should feel after that."

Honesty—his whole life spent alone so he never had to use it. With Walter, he had no other way.

Walter rolled so his face was pressed against Nate's bare chest. He turned just enough to rest his ear against Nate's pectoral, and he listened.

"My heartbeat?" Nate guessed.

"Beating like fury," Walter breathed. "That's amazing. All of that for me."

Nate laughed a little, palmed the back of Walter's head. "Yes," he said, his heart easing. A man who did not love him? Maybe. But it was looking less and less likely with every breath. "If you knew who I am, knew my faith, knew *me*, before this little house, you would know how very much I have become for you."

"I like it," Walter murmured. "I like who you are. Who you are with me. Stay like this. Stay like this, and I'll stay." He closed his eyes, and they lay, naked, letting the air cool their bodies in the breathless dark. Nate had a moment to hope—to pray even—that the Nazis really *would* wait until later, before his eyes closed in sleep.

ROCKS AND
WINDOW FRAMES

The room was dark and Nate was naked, and Walter was sitting on his chest, fully dressed, holding his hand over Nate's mouth.

"Someone hit our windowsill," Walter hissed. There was another sound, a short, sharp rap of rocks on wood.

Nate's heart raced, and he locked eyes with Walter, then darted his gaze to the window. One of them was going to have to go see.

Walter took his hand from Nate's mouth, and Nate whispered, "Let me look. She's seen me already. Go hide in the closet."

Walter opened his mouth to protest, and the next couple of rocks hit the window insistently. There was nothing for it. Walter had thought to bring Nate's clothes, and he dressed quickly, scanning through the slats of the window for one person, or two, or a platoon of Vichy soldiers ready to tear the house apart with howitzers. Nate longed for his pistol and wished Walter had thought to bring it when he'd gotten dressed. Of course, Nate had the feeling Walter had been dressed when the rocks had first hit the window frame anyway. They had been planning to spend some time outfitting the garage that night, after all.

Nate was half-terrified, half-relieved when the pale face appeared from the side of the house, distorted through the thin strips of light between the boards. There was no glass left, not in this window, and not for the first time, Nate wondered at Walter, cold and alone, huddling downstairs next to the wood stove in this palace of chilly winds.

Did he think of this house differently now?

"My boyfriend is coming tonight," the woman hissed. "What took you so long to hear me? He'll be here any minute!"

"We were sleeping so we might leave tonight," Nate hissed back unwisely. He was rattled by the question—they were sleeping, but sleeping naked, postcoital, and that was the last thing he wanted a stranger to know.

"Don't leave, stupid—*hide.* If you can just not get caught, I can get you to the signal. There's a contact scheduled in five days. You two just need to *stay out of sight.*" So Nate had been right—she *did* know the resistance who communicated with Hector's people. And Hector or someone like him would be flying a mission to listen for news in five days. Oh God. He could get them a plane.

"Well, if your boyfriend was not so excited he took the day off—"

"What can I say? I'm *very good*!" She spat the last part with viciousness, and Nate felt badly about baiting her.

"Do we have time to run to the garage?" he asked, and he could see the negative shake of her head.

"No. It's bright as day out—three quarters moon. He'll see you running. Hide inside—but don't move until daylight."

"I always wanted to be a fish in a barrel," Nate muttered, wondering if the idiom would translate.

"I'll try not to shoot you while I'm fucking a Nazi for my country!"

"I'm sorry," Nate said through the slat, immensely contrite. "Thank you."

She grunted in a distinctly masculine way. "Ugh, you are far too nice to be an American soldier. You must be a Jew. Is your companion as Jewish as you are?"

"Not even close, but his French is worse."

Her harsh laugh reassured him. "Excellent." Her voice softened. "Please, American. I have help for you. I will not turn you over to the pigs."

Nate tucked his shirt in and rolled up his cuffs, wondering how much of his undress she could see. "If I am alive tomorrow, I will believe you," he conceded. She rapped sharply on the windowsill and disappeared, and Nate turned to dismantle the bed.

He met Walter in the closet and shoved the folded—and soiled—linens onto the shelf on top of its more moth-eaten brethren.

Then Walter surprised him by opening up the plywood door and jumping down into a completely fashioned hole in the floor.

Nate wrinkled his nose in distaste. "How many insects are down here, do you think?"

"None," Walter said softly, matter-of-fact. "See this cloth I'm standing on? I used it to get rid of every creepy-crawly I could see. And look—" he indicated the two stools they'd been using about the house "—someplace to sit!"

Nate grinned at him. "Next time, we shall have to bring the cards too," he whispered genially. "Here, let me pull the wood over our heads."

This end of the house was elevated slightly by the stairs, so although the crawlspace was made close by the darkness, there was plenty enough room for the two of them to sit. Toward the front room, the boards above them dropped toward the foundation, leaving barely enough space for a man to lie flat. Under the closet, surrounded by water pipes, they were lucky indeed.

They were stowed neatly, two bugs in the corner of the drawer, when they heard the tromping up the porch stairs and that cheerful, lascivious voice echoing loudly through the house. "Nobody home *again*? Looks like we shall have to investigate!"

"Oh, Horst. The only thing you want to investigate is my dripping gash!"

Nate grimaced and peered at Walter by the thin light through the floorboards. He had his "no bullshit" eyebrow crooked. He might not have understood the banter, but he certainly got the gist. Sadly, it was the most sophisticated thing Horst had to say. The sex noises, loud and uninhibited, started again, and Nate had to give the girl (Horst called repeatedly for Ouida, so Nate was going to assume that was her name) credit: she *sounded* excited about the whole affair, even though he was reasonably sure she was not.

Seeing Nate's grimace, Walter leaned forward and whispered in his ear, "Why doesn't it sound as gross when *we're* doing it?"

Nate shoved his fist in his mouth and manfully tried to hold back his glare. Laughter threatened to choke him, and Walter didn't look the least repentant. This moment, deadly serious as it was, was suddenly high farce, and he squeezed his eyes shut in an effort to block out the noises and his sudden intense need to guffaw, which would give away their position and probably get them both killed.

He opened his eyes to the darkness, and Walter winked at him. Nate's head bumped up against the flooring, even sitting on the stool. He wanted to stretch, but he was afraid of making too much noise.

He was surprised and moved when Walter crab-walked toward him, setting the stool down close enough for Walter to lean against his side. Nate lifted his arm and wrapped it around Walter's shoulder, laying his cheek against his lover's clean, bright-orange hair. The laughter subsided, and the terror too. He closed his eyes, pictured the German officer discovering them, pictured surrendering to death, to the forgiving God he *hoped* existed, with serenity and grace. He was still afraid—he had so much he wanted to do, so many plans for that utopian moment embodied by "after the war"—but his heart quieted, and he no longer feared breaking into hysterical laughter that would undo them.

Behind his eyes, the moments with Walter painfully snapped like pictures in his mind, ran like a film, and he found himself thinking about his faith. *So, Leviticus says it was wrong. Leviticus also says we can sell our daughters into slavery. I would prefer not.*

Walter shifted against him, and Nate resisted the temptation to hold him so tight he couldn't breathe.

Ahava, *the love of passion. I would love Walter above any woman as Jacob loved Rachel more than Leah. There is no story that says that is wrong. I would love him as a partner and friend,* raya, *as my passion and lover,* ahava, *and bound to him in both loves, I would find* dod. *The* mishkav zakhar *we can keep to ourselves. And even that was lovely, ferocious and beautiful, the merging of bodies and hearts. Walter, I need to hear the words from you,* tateleh, *my faith is bound in words.*

But here, under the obscenity of sex and lusty screaming in their ears, there was no place for words.

Beside him, he felt Walter's tentative stretch, and he breathed deeply and silently, straightening his spine from the crouch on the stool. His body ached and cramped, and his breath—which had come easily enough when he was laboring inside Walter's body—was suddenly ruched under his ribs and contorting his body with pain.

"Sh," Walter whispered in his ear. "Getting loud."

Across the house, Ouida gave a gasp and a squeal, and Nate took a moment to hope that Horst was at least well-endowed. Not *all* of that noise should be feigned!

Can't breathe, Nate mouthed, and Walter straightened immediately. Nimbly, he hopped off the stool and sat, legs splayed in front of him. He patted his lap gingerly, and Nate took the hint. He got down heavily to his knees and stretched out, resting his head on Walter's thigh. The cramping in his chest eased, and breath came easier. Walter leaned back on one arm, and then, with the other hand, he began a soothing stroke of his fingers through Nate's unrecoverable hair. Gentle, sweet, the touch of a lover not a fellow sinner, Walter eased Nate's fears, his discomfort, his breathing.

Courtship, love—*not words until some woman from France brought them to England. Ahava, raya, dod, it boils down to this: one soul comforting another when ugly death surrounds us. I love you too, Walter. This touch, this is real.*

Later Nate would wonder how much time had passed. Did he and Walter make love for hours or minutes? Why did it feel as though years had passed with Ouida screaming above the floorboards?

Finally, finally, the noise quieted, and the sharp and acrid odor of tobacco filtered between the floorboards and through the house. Horst must have had more time this evening than the last, because there had been no moment for a cigarette before.

"So," Ouida said throatily on an exhale of smoke, "you have this evening off. Will you still have the next one or shall I be alone?"

Horst's laugh was low and filthy. "Oh, Ouida. I do not flatter myself that you are ever alone. No. Last time I was here with my dirty little screw, someone dosed the canteen with some sort of poison; the entire barracks got the runs and turned into blithering morons, missing the damned toilets."

"Ugh!" Ouida could have won awards as an actress. That sound was pure poetry. "What a hideous idea. True desperation, that."

"Yes, well, my commandant wanted his best lieutenant at the barracks for the next night, so my schedule changed." Horst was preening, bragging to a pretty girl in his bed. If the man would not have been inclined to kill them all without conscience, Nate might have felt bad for the deception.

"And you are such a man?" Ouida said playing coy. "Such a man that, should all hell break loose, the barracks would stand or fall for you?"

"I am," Horst answered smugly. "Just this morning, I found a man skulking at the edges of our barracks."

"*Oui*?" Ouida asked, nothing but casualness in her tone.

"*Oui*," Horst replied, his voice muffled, probably in her flesh.

"What did you do?"

"I had him shot, of course!" Horst laughed. "And when we searched the body, we found a Liberator on his person, so it was the right decision!"

"A Liberator?"

Nate, lying with his head pillowed on Walter's leg, struggled to sit upright.

"What?" Walter whispered.

Nate shook his head, unable to explain what he was thinking in a whisper. Instead, he sat and stared tensely at the damp brown boards on the underside of the floor.

"Yes, can you believe that? He comes to spy on an SS office with a one-shot gun?" There was the sound of a man spitting, and Nate's stomach clenched. "Stupid bastard. We shot him down like a dog."

"You didn't even question him?" Ouida asked, and something about her voice raised the hackles on Nate's neck.

She knew him. Oh God, she knew him.

Horst's voice sounded like he'd shrugged. "What was to learn? Diarrhea? Moved outhouses? Child's tricks."

Ouida's laugh was brittle and ugly, and Nate closed his eyes. This was not going to end well.

"They kept you from noticing the three planes' worth of guns and resistance soldiers that were dropped in that night," Ouida said, her voice suddenly frigid.

"Ouida? Is that a Lib—"

One shot. A one-shot gun.

One shot was all a woman needed to undo everything she'd striven for, and to violate the safety of make-believe Nate and Walter had carved from an abandoned house and need.

Walter jumped against him as the report rang out through the house, followed by the *thump* of a body. Ouida's shrieking, sobbing fury was not far behind. Nate stood and pushed against the displaced floorboards, and Walter helped him, both of them sniffing as the smell of gunpowder pervaded the house.

"What in the hell?" Walter asked, his voice sounding obscenely loud as they pulled themselves from under the floor and out of the closet. "He came, they fucked, they talked, she shot him?"

"He told her he'd killed someone," Nate filled in, wondering how much Walter had understood with his limited knowledge of French. "I'm thinking she knew who it was."

They treaded quietly but quickly, unsure what they would encounter when they broached the front room.

A flashlight illuminated the room, giving the forms and shadows a freakish edge. Ouida was standing, naked and debauched, in the middle of the room, the gun still clutched in her hand. Horst—apparently—was on his stomach, as though he'd gone to roll off the couch and had been shot before he could get up. The hole in his head was nearly as big as an orange, shattered bone, gray matter, blood, all of it a mangle around the dead man's once-plain, high-cheekboned face, and Nate couldn't look at it for long.

Instead, he concentrated on Ouida, who was weeping, clenching the gun and grinding it into her forehead.

"Walter, *tateleh*," he said, using English without thinking, "go get her a blanket please. We need to calm her down."

Walter glanced sharply at him but trotted down the hall anyway, and Nate took stock of the situation. Of all things, what surprised him was the smell.

Directly under the smell of the cigarettes and the gunpowder was the smell of the wood stove and the rabbit they'd stored in the cupboard for their next day's lunch.

"It's just as well," he said to Ouida in French. "He would have smelled our dinner if you'd stayed here much longer. One way or another, the man had to die."

"Gerard," she mumbled brokenly. "We were friends in school. Always, always he followed me and Everard. He was supposed to observe, nothing else. Poor boy." She dropped the gun then, useless now that she'd used the shot. "Poor, poor boy." Without mercy, she glared at the man she'd killed, close enough to spit soundly on his corpse as his blood saturated the couch cushion and pooled on the floor below. "Pig!" She spat again. "Fucking pig! Your cock was tiny, you fucking pig! It was like screwing my little finger!"

"Oh, and that is information I never wanted," Nate said good-naturedly, taking the sheet from Walter and wrapping it around her shoulders. "But here, sweet girl. You need to wrap up and get dressed, and then we need to dispose of the body here in the woods."

Ouida shivered in the confines of the sheet and looked up at both of them, seemingly stunned.

"Why dispose of the body?" she asked. "You two are going to need to leave this place anyway!"

"Yes, my dear," Nate said, thinking as fast as he could, "but if he is found fully dressed in the woods, this will be an act of war, and they will search for *men*, but if they find him naked in this house—"

"They will know it was me," she filled in, voice wooden. "I am so *stupid*. Yes. Yes, I understand." She shook herself, trying to get her bearings. "You two, take him out into the woods—this is a good plan. With any luck the scavengers," she spat, "will have eaten most of him before they can find him. I will clean up here. Try to erase your presence." She scented the air. "Is that *rabbit* I smell?" Then, absurdly, "I'm hungry. In fact, I'm *ravenous*. Can I eat some of that?"

"Really?" Nate asked, incredulous. He met eyes with Walter who was listening to the two of them alertly. "She wants to eat our dinner."

Walter's eyes widened. "Of course. Tell her to make herself at home. Save some for us, since we never got to it. And we're going to . . .?"

"Dress the dead man and hide him out in the woods."

Walter didn't spare any surprise for that plan. "Of course we are. Damn it, we should have just stayed there until this whole thing blew over."

Nate grimaced at him. "When the sun rises, Walter, the SS will be all over this place—bedroom, bathroom, beneath the house. I think our time here is at an end."

Walter's mouth twisted in what Nate would later think of as grief. "That is too damned bad," he said, his face pinched and unhappy. "I could have played make-believe here my entire life."

Nate closed his eyes. "The bells," he said, hoping Walter would remember. "The bells, they will chime for both of us."

Walter nodded, a wistful smile on his face. "Yeah, well, I guess that's the best we can hope. C'mon, Nate, we need to get this guy back in his slick officer duds so nobody thinks he got lucky."

Dressing a dead body was a ghastly business. The flesh was warm but cooling and flaccid—it had give but no life. They struggled, and when they were done, they realized they'd forgotten his undershorts. Ouida found them stuffed between couch cushions and told Nate she'd use them to clean the blood off the floor. Perhaps the man's state of undress wouldn't be noticed, or, if it was, would be considered a sign of a perversion.

"He deserves to be reviled," she said viciously, and Nate wouldn't argue with her.

He grabbed under Horst's arms, and Walter grabbed his hastily laced boots, and together they hauled him out of what had once been their home.

The trip through the woods was miserable—not quite chilly, but there was no path, no light, no landmarks. Nate found a constellation in the sky he recognized and guided himself by that star. When they had labored until they were sweaty and breathless and the house was out of sight, they dropped the SS officer's body without comment, then turned and made their way back, grimly. No prayer for this man.

Even the most wicked spent very little time in Gehinnom; this man would get no help from Nate to venture to the gates of Gan Eden.

The trip back was faster, making Nate wish they'd gone a little farther in disposing of the body, but the night was getting on. Sighting the clearing with the rutted path and almost invisible road to the summer cottage made them both stop. In the moonlight, the house looked eerily familiar, as though they had lived there for years rather than camped out there for a month and a half.

"I'll miss it," Walter said quietly. They were still standing in the shadows thrown by the moon, and Nate seized his hand and pulled him behind a tree out of sight from the house. Walter's usual self-sufficiency was temporarily missing, and he looked up at Nate with the trusting expression of a lost child.

"We will have a home," Nate promised him, almost desperately. "We will survive the war and find each other in New York on New Year's Eve. We will get a small house and make a living, and people will think, 'Oh, what nice men. It's a shame they never married. A Jew and a gentile—what good friends they seem to be.'"

Walter grinned wickedly, and for all the years after, that was the picture in the album Nate pulled out most often. Wicked and hopeful, ready to have faith in a dream when, as far as Nate could tell, he'd never had faith in anything at all.

"Only you and me'll have to know what happens when the lights go out, right?"

"We shall keep a separate bedroom," Nate assured him soberly. "And tell everyone it is yours."

Walter cackled, the sound ringing in the moonlight like church bells, and Nate captured his mouth then, hopeful, oh so hopeful, that he could make it happen. Walter responded, warm and wet, and welcoming, and for the first time, Nate fell into him, trusting that Walter had caught him and that they were falling together. They separated at the same time, and Nate touched Walter's cheek, and then they turned toward the house.

The hope kept them going.

Ouida was washed and dressed when they returned, and if she had found anything in the house that she disapproved of, nothing about her demeanor showed it.

Nate used the old blankets to bundle a change of clothes for each of them, the playing cards, and the most recent batch of bagels and crackers, slightly stale, which he wrapped in a torn strip of linen first. The film he pocketed in his flight jacket, which he rolled up in the pack with the shaving kit, and his sidearm he shoved into the back of the slacks he'd borrowed from the castoffs in the garage.

He was double-checking the entire thing when Walter came in, looking forlorn.

He had the book in one hand and the doll in the other.

"I don't suppose . . ."

Nate was going to say yes. He wanted them both—their book, their doll, their pretend life—but Ouida walked into the bedroom in that moment and rolled her eyes.

"Are you defective? We're tramping through woods for at least five miles if we don't want to waltz through the barracks. The flight jacket, I can understand, but a child's *book*!"

Walter looked at Nate sickly, apparently reading Ouida's tone if not her actual words. He dropped both things so quickly, they slithered off the bed, and Nate winced when he heard the tinkle of porcelain.

New Year's Eve, he mouthed, wondering if Walter could do this. His unit, the trainload of prisoners, his lover—they'd all been taken away. Could he leave this place too?

But Walter had always been tough. Nate would remember that in later years when he pulled these mental pictures out like a worn love letter, all of them—the good and the bad, the pouting, the coldness, the reluctance to believe. All these snapshots would be precious, perfect in their imperfection, because they were all Nate had.

In this moment, Walter glared at Ouida with some serious dislike, and then, face hard and determined, nodded at Nate.

"We don't got any alcohol or gas or anything. I'm gonna drag some dry brush in, and we can torch the place that way."

Nate nodded. "Good thinking."

"New Year's Eve," Walter said briefly, and like that, it was their code.

He turned and stalked out, and Nate bent, ignoring Ouida, and picked up the doll. Her face and head were not, in fact, damaged. Only her foot, which might easily be repaired. Glaring at Ouida, he tucked the doll into the pack.

"She doesn't weigh much," he said quietly. "I would very much love to bring her."

Ouida shrugged, indifferent. "We are going around the village, and I am stowing you in a barn near the field where they make their drops. If they send a plane for you, it can land there. You two will have to stay *in the barn* during the day and hold your water until the small hours of the dark. The old man will come and go, but he relies on his son for the top loft, and François won't be by until after the operative calls down the plane. You should be safe. But the barn is very visible in the light, and animals make noise."

Nate nodded. "The OSS operative will be picked up with us?"

"I am not sure." Ouida shrugged. "Perhaps not. His cover is safe."

"Food?"

"I can bring you some but not often. I will leave you with water, but the old man has cows. I suggest you make do."

Nate grimaced at the thought of the poor cow being subjected to his ministrations, but it was sustenance and shelter when, very shortly, they would have none.

"Do you think the forest will catch around the house?" he asked, suddenly fearful. He was relieved when Ouida shook her head.

"The ground is moist, and you've seen the runoff streams. A few leagues to the north, those get bigger—they'll control any burn. Besides, there's enough ventilation in the house itself. It will burn fast and hot, but localized. Don't worry. We had planned to burn it down when Horst had outlived his usefulness anyway."

"We?" he asked, and abruptly the thought of putting his and Walter's fate in this woman's hands frightened him.

"Me, my brother Everard, and my lover, Emile."

"A lover?" Nate looked at her, shocked. It was one thing to do what she'd been doing with Horst as an agent of the resistance but quite another when your lover knew.

"How many members of *your* family have the Nazis killed?" she asked, voice dripping with venom.

"My uncle's family, I assume," Nate told her, his blood running cold. He had forgotten, hadn't he? In his moments with Walter, in the quest for the healing at the end of the war, he'd forgotten about what the war had taken away, *was* taking way, as every minute passed by and he frolicked in the woods.

"Well, then you know," she said dismissively. "Emile will give anything to destroy them. Even me."

Nate grunted in assent, but he didn't understand. He wouldn't have given Walter. They had never used the word *desertion*, but he knew that he'd at least thought about giving his freedom, his liberty in his home country to keep things with Walter as they were.

Love, he thought. *I have more in me than hate.*

Simplistic. And not true. He would learn that hatred was a matter of the things that had been taken away. Once there was nothing left to love, hate was all that was left to feel.

He folded his makeshift pack then and slung it over his back. When he and Ouida reached the bottom of the stairs, Walter was standing in the sitting room by a pile of brush, trying hard not to look at the SS officer's spattered blood.

"We ready?" he muttered.

Walter nodded and struck a match from the book he'd been using for the stove. A whiff of sulfur, a flare of light, and the tinder caught. Walter and Nate met eyes once, and then Walter turned around and started down the stone steps and into the clearing, Nate and Ouida on his tail.

FIELDS OF GOLD

The glow of the burning house illuminated their way for a couple of miles, but that was the only break they caught. When the warm yellow light of their destructing home had faded behind them, they discovered that woods by moonlight were lovely and dangerous. As when they were depositing the body, every step was a struggle around underbrush, clumps of vegetation, and holes of rinsed away earth with root structures rising above to trip the unwary. More than once, Nate steadied Ouida or Walter as their shorter legs made negotiating the terrain more difficult. More than once, Nate found himself falling back to walk side by side with Walter, only to respond to Ouida's request that he come forward and talk to her.

Asking for Nate's opinion was one thing, but as of yet, she hadn't so much as looked Walter in the eyes or acknowledged his presence. Nate wasn't sure if it was the officer distinction, or Walter's diminutive height—or even the bright orange of his hair. At their first rest stop, she called Nate forward and offered him a drink from a canteen that she'd apparently stolen from Horst. Nate turned to offer it to Walter, and she tried to snatch it out of Nate's hand.

Nate jerked it away and gave it to Walter, ignoring her sniff of derision.

He'd hoped that had been the end of it, but apparently Walter decided to deal with it in his own inimitable way.

"Officer," she called softly as the darkness around them softened, "come see."

Nate grimaced at Walter, who glared at the back of Ouida's head.

"She speak English?" he asked, his voice gritty.

"I don't know," Nate answered, suddenly wondering. She could very well know but be keeping the conversation in French to exclude Walter. "But I think she thinks I'm in command."

"Does she know I think she's a vicious murdering bitch who has her sights on my man?" Walter spat, and in front of them, Ouida stopped abruptly and gasped.

Nate turned to Walter and stared, shocked that he would risk, well, *everything*, in a spate of jealousy, and he realized that Walter wasn't seeing him at all.

Walter and Ouida were locking eyes, and Nate realized that Ouida, indeed, must know some English.

Instinctively, Nate took a step in front of Walter and intercepted Ouida's glower.

She flushed under his defensive gaze.

"I understand more English than I speak," she conceded. "Tell him that I was talking to you as an officer. I assumed you were the leader."

"I am," Nate replied. "An officer, that is. Walter is very much his own man."

She looked away. "According to him, so are you."

Nate didn't pretend not to know what she was talking about. "If I am, does that mean we don't get your shelter and the plane? Because I assure you, the film I need to bring to Naval Intelligence is still very much as relevant as it was when you thought I could be yours."

Ouida raised her eyebrows. "For all I know—"

"We have proven ourselves nothing but trustworthy," Nate said shortly. "The same can't be said for yourself."

He didn't like this. She was frightening and unpredictable, and they were relying on her because she claimed to know the OSS operative that Nate knew was here. He had no idea who it could be, and he didn't blend in well enough to ask. Neither did Walter. But *oy*! The sight of her, naked, in front of a dead man, costing him and Walter their only shelter in hostile territory because she couldn't maintain for one more week the charade she'd started—that was hard to shake.

And he didn't like the way she treated Walter.

Nate stared at Ouida for a few more moments, refusing to back down. Finally, she bit her lip and broke eye contact.

"You were very kind," she said into the silence. "Forgive me if I misinterpreted."

Nate shrugged. "You wanted to show me something? Dawn is breaking—if we're to be hidden before the farmer gets here, we need to hurry."

She nodded and swallowed. "Yes. This stream here. It will be your source of water." Stooping, she filled the canteen and passed it back to Nate. "Take care of that. You won't get a chance to fill it up again until tonight."

"Thank you," he said, remaining slightly suspicious.

Ouida grimaced. "I am not going to have you shot for being queer," she said after a pause, seemingly ashamed. "I truly am grateful."

Nate sighed, letting it go. They would live or they would die—he was exhausted, his chest hurt, and Walter had stumbled more than walked for the past few miles—and he would have to trust Ouida because they had no choice. He would have to let her be human to them, and believe in sanctuary and succor, or wander the countryside behind enemy lines.

"And now, so are we," he said with a weary smile. "So the farmhouse . . .?"

"Follow this stream, for a league. You should make it before Monsieur Gaubert arises to feed the cows."

"Where will you be going?" Nate asked, concerned.

Ouida bit her lip, appearing every bit as tired as Nate felt. "I need to tell Emile and my brother about Gerard. And we need to find another way to distract the soldiers in the barracks in five days. Horst was a pig, but he was right. He was the most competent officer in the compound. If they are stirred up like a hornet's nest, or too suspicious, keeping them away from the drop zone will be much more difficult."

Nate remembered what Horst had said about stomach difficulties and moved outhouses. "Where *did* you get the idea to distract them with diarrhea and mysteriously moving outhouses?"

Ouida stared at him as though he were mad. "Why, from the operative at the OSS, the one who broadcasts from the plane. He said they have a room full of people just coming up with things to do that will terrorize the Nazis!"

Nate laughed shortly, and she pointed toward the stream again. "Follow the stream, and be quick about it. Either Emile or I should be here tomorrow morning, about this hour, in this place. You can stretch your legs, get food and water, and then go back to hiding. God be with you, Officer."

Nate nodded at her. Brave girl, no matter where her loyalties lay. "And you. Good night, Ouida. We shall see you again."

Without a look back, Nate and Walter resumed their side-by-side trudge along the stream.

Nate had been born in the city and needed Walter's reassurances that the cows in the field they walked through would not hold grudges.

"Never seen cows before, city boy?" Walter asked, shoving aside a massive flank.

"Not quite this personally," Nate conceded. There was a small roan who thought Nate was her particular friend. He found he needed to push at her fine-boned face more than once.

"Well, this farmer's lucky it's so warm this year. If there was still dew on the grass when the cows were out, he'd be risking worms, and that's a horrible thing. My daddy lost half his herd to them fuckers one year."

"So many things I didn't know about," Nate said, smiling. He tripped on a hummock of grass and caught himself on a cow. The cow didn't bear any ill will.

The barn was as big as Ouida had promised, and it loomed in front of the sunrise. Nate could see the door in the side. In spite of the awfulness of the night, he was suddenly loath to venture into the promised shelter.

"We saw the sunset last night," he said, not sure which moment was the illusion.

"Yeah. That feels weird as all hell, you know that?"

"Most assuredly. Your life can change in a night, in a minute, in a month."

"In a plane crash," Walter said grimly, and Nate, chest aching, breath coming almost too hard to talk, had to smile.

"Let us hope we don't need another plane crash for it to change for the better," he muttered, and the two of them dragged their ragged persons into the barn and up the ladder into the loft. Nate had the presence of mind to unfold the blanket so they were not lying on straw, and they pillowed their heads on his flight jacket, which was only nominally better than being flat.

Sleep claimed them so brutally, it was the next best thing to death.

The next few days were uncomfortable, claustrophobic, and terrifying.

They were also sometimes filled with quiet wonder.

They awoke late in the afternoon of the first day to the sound of old Mr. Gaubert talking to his cows. At first they were frightened—afraid that he was talking to someone in the barn who represented danger—and then Nate heard something that sounded very like, "Get your big tit-bag out of my way, you misbegotten bovine!" and had to stifle laughter against Walter's arms.

They waited in breathless silence until the old man stomped out of the barn, slamming the door behind him. Nate leaned over and whispered a translation in Walter's ear, and the feeling of Walter laughing silently against his chest charmed a moment that should have been fraught with fear.

They lay there, still and quiet as mice for the next few hours, but that didn't mean they didn't communicate. Nate lifted his hands over his head to stretch after a moment, raising his face to the sun streaming in the high loft window, closing his eyes against the hay-colored dust. Walter passed his hand over the plane of Nate's stomach, slowly, so slowly Nate could feel every callus on the pads of Walter's fingers and his palm. It was not a sexual touch, per se, but it was . . . sensual.

Nate kept his hands under his head, allowing his stomach to rise and fall with the warmth of Walter's hand against his ribs. He cocked his head and grinned, and Walter smiled shyly in return.

Breath, breath, breath, the weight of Walter's palm steady on his body. Nate blinked and nodded, and that was the signal. Walter rolled to his back fully and stretched, and Nate did the same thing. He closed his eyes for a moment, feeling that silky skin and the stringy muscles. Walter breathed out sharply through his nose, and Nate moved his hand softly up, framing Walter's throat just to feel his pulse.

Walter closed his eyes and put his hand on top of Nate's. Nate lost track of the moments they continued this way, silently touching each other, not to arouse but just to feel the other's pulse, breath, and skin.

But the arousal was always there, intention or not, simmering just underneath the surface.

At nightfall, when the shadows crept down, dimming the single window, they heard the farmer stomping away, muttering one last curse at the cows. It was Walter's turn to lay with his hand along Nate's stomach, and as soon as the door closed, he met Nate's eyes and smiled that shy smile that Nate had become used to with their tenderness in bed.

Without a word—because they were unused to speaking by now, their mouths gummy, throats dusty with only a few gulps of water to sustain them throughout the day—he undid Nate's belt and his trousers and slid his hand underneath the waistband.

His hand on Nate's cock was enormous, the fist of doom, shaking the earth. It engulfed all of Nate's body, strong and hard, warm and safe; it became all of Nate's world. He closed his eyes against the splintered boards of the loft, against the bales upon bales of hay, and breathed in warm animal, the spring-verdant earth outside, the musk and unapologetic sweat of the man who held Nate's life in his palm.

Walter stroked without finesse, but then, none was needed. The burn of their desire had been in every quiet touch, every indrawn breath, every moment when their eyes had met and they'd tried desperately to read each other's mind. A few dozen harsh breaths, strokes of Nate's cock being both caressed and abused, and he gasped, the lights behind his eyes an acidic red and green, and climax swept his body with naked claws.

At his side, Walter fumbled and then covered the head with a rough cloth, and Nate had no help for it but to spurt, spilling semen into Walter's hand and the dirty linen he'd apparently wadded in his pocket during their hasty exit from the summer cabin.

For the next few minutes, Nate held his hand to his chest to keep his heart from leaping out, and Walter cleaned him roughly. When he was done, he tucked Nate's manhood back behind the placket of his trousers, did his belt, and met Nate's eyes in the fallen darkness.

"We should go to the stream," he said softly.

Nate nodded and palmed the back of Walter's head, pulling him to his sweaty chest. "Yes," he agreed, because it was time. "But tomorrow, it's your turn."

"I wouldn't object to that." One corner of Walter's mouth was twisted up in a smirk Nate found truly endearing. He ran his finger over that corner of his mouth.

I had never dreamed of being in love. I did not know the mechanics, the nuts and bolts, the quirk of lips, the texture of skin, the dimension of another's hands upon my body. Forgive me, Father. I did not know you made this thing as vast as the sky, so that we may see the sky and not tremble.

"Good," Nate whispered. "I shall enjoy it."

Walter scrambled to the hay ladder, and the moment ended, became one of the pocketful of them that Nate would finger smooth like river pebbles in the years to come.

There was no one at the stream that night to greet them with food or news, so they had no choice. They relieved themselves and drank copiously, then relieved themselves again. Reluctantly, as dawn approached, they refilled the canteen and ventured back to the barn. Nate spotted some carrots hanging by the door of the one horse stall and snagged them on his way up the ladder. He got to the top of the loft and realized Walter was missing.

"Wal—" He choked off his words at the distant sound of voices—the old man and someone else—and searched wildly around the barn. He spotted that bright-orange head, low and practically hidden by the largest, most fertile of the bovines, and felt his bowels loosen, as empty as they were.

"Walter!" he hissed furiously, and Walter glared up at him, holding what appeared to be a half-filled milk bucket.

"That's wonderful. Get your scrawny body up the fucking ladder!"

Walter's eyes opened widely—surprised by the blasphemy probably—and he stood up and slid between cow bodies to get out of the stall. He was halfway to the ladder when he heard the old man's voice rise querulously, and Nate draped himself over the edge of the hayloft to take the bucket so Walter could climb faster.

For his entire life, Nate would wonder how he hadn't simply died of terror in those moments. They heard the voices, they heard the old man: *he was coming* and someone else with him, someone with a sharp, snarly voice speaking French with a German accent.

In fear and desperation, Nate threw his flight jacket on top of the milk bucket and then scattered straw over it. Walter had scrambled up, and together they lay on their stomachs on the wool blanket and covered themselves with hay. Nate had just pulled what felt like half a bale over their heads and was wondering if either one of them could breathe when they heard the muffled sound of the door opening, and the argument that had been outside snarled its way in.

"I'm telling you, there is no resistance in these parts," the old man said. "You can search my barn all you want, but all you'll find is cows and shit. Feel free to take some of the shit with you."

There was the click of a Beretta, and the old man's high-pitched voice tinged bright with fear.

"Now listen to me, old man. We are missing the one officer in my barracks who could find his cock in the dark. I don't care which of you maggots is responsible—be they resistance, puling cattle, it makes no difference to me. But if I find out that you or *anybody* concealed the whereabouts of the fucker who made him disappear, I shall watch your brains spatter across the barn, do you hear me?"

There was a sharp report then, loud enough to frighten the cows into lowing, and the old man cried out despairingly. "*Gertrude*! She was my best milker; without her I cannot feed my family!"

"You should do what civilized people do," the officer snarled. "Eat steak." The gun sounded again, several times, but since the cows continued their terrified lowing and the old man's wailing was still loud and pitiful, Nate had to contain his panic. It was cruel, meant to terrorize, nothing more. In the fury of the firing, Walter's hand crept into his, and he felt water slide along his nose, saturating the wool blanket beneath his face.

Terrorizing tactics. Well, yes, they were working.

There was a pause then, and Nate had to force himself to breathe, slowly and with great restraint. The sound of booted feet echoed hollowly on the floorboards of the barn, even muffled by the straw, and the cows, apparently, were frightened into silence. For a moment, there was nothing, no sound but the petty god who held their life and death in his hands.

There was another moment, and then the creaking sound of the ladder straining under the weight of a body. Some grunts, some prodding of the straw—Nate could hear these things but he was too busy holding his breath to worry that his own pile of straw was moving. Underneath his hip and his stomach, he felt a seeping wetness, and his heart stalled. *Oh God.* What if Walter had been hit? What if after all of this, Walter had been randomly killed by fire meant to do nothing but frighten an old man?

The wetness continued to seep, and then the smell of ammonia made the space under the straw even closer and more strangling.

Walter's hand squeezed his, and he let more tears slip by.

We are both frightened, Walter. I'll never mention it. If we survive to live side by side, it will be as though you never dropped your water and I never cried.

He remembered Walter saying once that he'd fallen asleep while the Nazis were searching the house because if they were going to find him, he could have missed that part without worry. He was not sure how long they lay, faces pressed against the wool, Walter's urine seeping through their clothes, but he did feel a moment of slipping away, of almost peace, exhaustion slowing his heart, relaxing his muscles. He didn't tense when that heavy, jackbooted body thumped down the ladder, and he barely blinked when the barn door slammed, leaving only the weeping old man, the restless livestock, and the visceral blood and shit smell of the murdered cow.

They lay there quiet for the rest of the day, and Nate simply drifted. Below them, the farmer's family and friends engaged in a flurry of activity, hauling out the murdered cow to butcher so that they might at least have the meat, and cleaning the blood out of the stall. It took many people, all of them bemoaning the Nazis and railing against the rebels who were trying to get them killed.

On the one hand, he felt a lingering guilt: he had been—no matter how inadvertently—a part of the instrument to bring vengeance on these people. On the other hand, he felt a simmering anger. There were so many brave men and women facing death, making sacrifices—what was worse? To lose the cow to a senseless murder, or to sacrifice a cow *knowing* that what you were doing was saving the lives of two men who were part of the effort to help?

But then, even Nate couldn't put anything more specific than "war effort" to the tenuous connection between the film in his pocket and the life of the farmer's cow.

It was a tangle, and the best thing that could be said about it was that it kept him hypnotized and in his own head for the better part of the day. Finally, as darkfall began to tinge the inside of the barn, the last of the family and friends cleared out.

Nate and Walter waited until full dark, until they heard nothing but the lowing of cattle and chirping of crickets, before they squeezed each other's hands and struggled to a sitting position as though they'd worn a stack of bricks on their bodies instead of straw.

Nate rustled in the straw and came back with Walter's change of clothes. Walter did the same and returned with the carrots and the milk. He sniffed experimentally and then let Nate sniff.

"I . . ." Nate's tongue cleaved to the roof of his mouth, and he realized he hadn't been able to swallow for hours. He took a swig from the canteen and passed the water to Walter. "I don't think it turned," Nate said after a moment of swishing the water around his mouth. "I think the jacket and the straw must have kept it insulated."

Walter nodded and sipped experimentally, then gulped, as though he couldn't help it. Nate tapped him on the shoulder, not so much because he was craving milk for his own but because he was pretty sure Walter would make himself sick. Walter put the bucket down and went for the carrots next, and Nate took his turn with the milk bucket. After a few moments, they were no longer light-headed, but their hearts were still as heavy as they had been.

"I have got to fuckin' wash and change," Walter said after a pause.

"I'll bring the blanket too," Nate murmured. "It's as though you read my mind."

They were silent on the trek to the creek, both of them mindful that it was much earlier this evening than it had been the last. They found a quiet, deep place in the stream—but one with moving water—and undressed, washing and wringing their soiled clothes first and their bodies second. When they were done, they sat naked on a flat rock and met each other's eyes.

"If the fucking Nazis find us now, I'll drown myself," Walter said after a moment, and for no logical reason whatsoever, that struck Nate as high comedy. He snickered, choking the sound against his hand, and it wasn't enough. He ended up laughing silently against his upper arm, shoulders shaking, eyes streaming with tears.

Walter held his cupped hands up to his face, trying to keep himself from letting the noise out. One heel beat a fruitless tattoo against the side of the rock.

Nate wasn't sure either one of them could stop. With a gasp, he jumped back into the water and watched, relieved, as Walter did the same. After a deep breath, he submerged himself fully and came back up for air, and when Walter emerged from his own dunking, Nate held out his arms.

"I need to hold you," he said, completely sober.

Walter nodded, and that's all there was for a moment: Walter's body in his arms, their bare skin touching in the cool water.

They separated after a moment—so much danger, even in a stream in the middle of the night. After that, there was nothing to do but to hang their clothes and blanket up for a cursory drying and to crouch in the shadows, waiting for someone who may or may not come.

"If someone comes," Nate whispered, "let me talk to him. Stay in hiding."

"I'm not a coward," Walter snarled.

Nate grunted in irritation. "I'm an officer, damn it. Me, they'll capture. You, they'll execute."

Walter's sigh was eloquent and defeated. "I'd rather die than hide like this anymore."

"Don't say that!" Nate's voice rose sharply, and Walter rapped him equally sharply on the arm. "Don't say that," Nate hissed, not willing to give up.

"I need you to live," Walter murmured, and he sounded done in, too done in to have an emotion-fraught conversation in the dark. "But that's about the only thing I've got the strength to need."

They were sitting in the shadows of the underbrush, waiting for the night to pass. Nate shoved himself back against the tree a little more firmly and took Walter's hand.

"Sleep, Walter," he said softly. He looked up at the full moon and wondered what day it was. He'd crashed in early March—surely Passover had come and gone. Had his parents given away all of their unwanted food the day before, to the non-Jews they knew? Would they give that food to Walter and expect him to be grateful? Had they opened the doors on the third glass of wine? Had they told the story of the four brothers—the Wise, the Wicked, the Simple, and the Young?

Walter's breathing fell into an exhausted rhythm next to him, and Nate wondered almost despairingly which brother he would be. Once, he'd thought he was the Wise. He knew the traditions, he respected them, but he was practical too, knew when to blend in.

But this thing with Walter . . . it had become all of his being. Was he Wicked, turning his back on this part of his faith? Was he Simple, believing that the one section of Leviticus had no meaning? Or was he merely Young, naive to believe that love could be so important that God would love it in all its forms?

He didn't know. He knew he missed the Seder feast—never again would he take for granted a full plate or a cup of wine. Never again would he take for granted his family—repressive father, vain mother. Who was he to judge? They had toasted his health with wine in a time when wine and all things were hard to come by. The world around him had been getting their hands dirty for food, and somehow his parents had reminded him that every hard-earned scrap of it had been a blessing.

The Seder feast was a reminder of the things his people had been deprived of, and of how to remember that a home and plenty were not to take as a given.

Nate had taken his home and his plenty for granted. But then, men like him and Walter were always destined to be cast out at the feast, weren't they?

My people painted lamb's blood on our doors so God would not take out his wrath on our sons. Walter would have been left out in the cold. Or his was the blood that would have been painted on the doors. He is innocent, oh God. He is the Young. He is the Young, and he needs our protection, and Wise, Wicked, or Simple, I am all he has.

Around dawn, he heard the crackle of branches and the sibilance of a French accent. "American! American, are you here? My sister, Ouida, sent me."

Nate had been covered in fear and sweating in urine all day—the instinct to stay hidden and say nothing was almost stronger than his hunger.

"American, I helped clean up François's cow this afternoon. You were brave to stay silent, but now that I have some of that cow cooked, it would be foolish not to show yourself."

Nate's stomach, which had sat silently all day, eating its own lining in the acid of fear, suddenly spoke up, and the voice gave a gentle chuckle.

"Ouida said you were cagey. But we missed you last night, and your schedule has moved up. Please . . . this could be the only food you get until the plane lands."

"It would be a shame to miss that," Nate said quietly, leaving his hiding place. "Poor Gertrude." As far as Nate could tell, Walter stayed fast asleep.

"Ah, you *are* here." At last, Nate could put a face to the voice, and, yes, he looked very like his sister—dark curling hair, full lips, soft brown eyes, and delicate features.

"It would seem," Nate said, smiling as best he could. Standing, he could actually smell the cooked meat, and his body was remembering that mostly unspoiled milk and carrots did not really sustain it for that much fear.

"My sister said there was another one. He's not—"

"No!" Nate muttered quickly. "No. He is fine, but I am letting him sleep. It has not been . . ."

"Yes," the young man murmured. "I understand. I'm Everard. Pleased to meet you."

Nate met the young man's hand and remembered who he was. For the first time in over a month, he introduced himself as, "Lieutenant Nathan Meyer, US Air Force. Pleased to meet you."

Everard nodded, as though this was the man he'd expected, which should have amused Nate. It was, in fact, the last young man he had thought he'd be.

"I understand you have something of value to the OSS. Ouida was thin on details, but our operative needs to know how important this mission is. Landing in a cow field isn't a picnic, even in the middle of nowhere as Provence Claire La Lune."

"Film," Nate said, and in this silver-and-black moment, it seemed a miracle to him that he'd taken the pictures, had kept them with him through the wreck, recovery, their precipitate flight through the woods. A whim, and it had wrecked his plane. A dogged obsession, and it had made him important enough to rescue.

An accident of duty, and it had saved Walter's life.

"They are building something, I think," he said truthfully. "Somewhere they are not expected to be. That is the only reason I can think of that they chased my plane so hard to shoot it down. They left Stuttgart unprotected, and Strasbourg too. It was not my first mission; those dogfighters were worried."

Everard nodded. "Good. I will not ask you where the film is. We will assume it is hidden back in the barn. We need you two gone as much as you need to go, and this operative . . . he's stingy with the favors."

Nate nodded, then said, "Tell them my name—and that I'm a friend of Hector's—this may still be his outpost. I know it was his job to talk to the operatives from the air."

Everard's eyes lit up. "That is excellent news! We shall get you and your sleeping friend a plane out of here yet!"

"Good," Nate said shortly. "I would hate to cost your people any more cows."

An awkward silence descended. "Well, at least the cows are tasty, no?" With that, Everard passed over the packet of food that was making Nate weak with the smell alone.

"At this point, tree bark is tasty," Nate agreed, but his voice softened. "Thank you. Should we try to meet tomorrow?"

"Yes. Emile wanted to meet you. Ouida can't stop talking about the brave, kind Americans."

Nate's mouth watered, and his head ached as he restrained himself from diving into the food packet; even so, he detected a note of bitterness in Everard's voice.

"These 'brave, kind Americans' were hiding in a cabin in the woods. We'd still be there, trying to decide what to do if your sister hadn't at least told us the name of your province. I take pictures, Everard. I don't even fly the plane."

"But you know how?" Everard goaded, and Nate had to concede to the cursory time in flight school.

"*Oui.*"

"Then why the modesty?"

"My friend fought in Africa and lost his entire unit. I'm late to this war."

Everard made an indeterminate sound. "Yes, well, you're American. It's your lot in life."

Wonderful. But he sounded less bitter, so perhaps they could live with each other in the time it took for Nate and Walter to make it to safety.

The sky was lightening now, and although it was earlier than it had been the day before, that had been too close for comfort. As one, they looked at that terrifying light and nodded. Everard made a little bow and melted into the forest.

Nate waited until he was gone and went to wake Walter.

Walter was pale in the shadows, shaking with cold and fatigue as he woke.

"Here," Nate said gently, his own hands shaking with the need for it. "I have food."

The meat was wedged between great, thick pieces of bread, and there were two apples, sound and sweet, with them. Nate ripped the sandwich in half and shoved the apples in his pocket.

"We should eat the meat and bread now; the smell will be out of place in the barn."

"Ugh. Too big a portion."

Nate was nearly done with his part, his stomach appeased but not full. It was a Seder feast to him, but he was beyond savoring it.

"Eat," he urged through a full mouth. "Eat. We need to be strong for the days ahead."

Walter grimaced and folded half his food back up in the wrapper. "You eat it for me," he muttered apologetically. "Or save it. Maybe under the hay, no one will smell it."

Nate put the wrapped package under his shirt and made Walter drink more from the canteen. Then they both relieved themselves for the last time that night and walked back to the barn.

There were no Nazis in the barn this time, no prematurely slaughtered cows. But there was no lovemaking either. This time, when the farmer stumped out for the last time that day, Nate turned to Walter to find him curled in a ball, shivering. Nate draped over his back and spent the next few hours whispering in his ear, trying to give him enough safety to rest. He slept, limp, exhausted, and Nate feared very likely sick, until it was time to go meet their contact. Nate was tempted to skip the meeting. He had to force Walter to eat the remainder of the food, and he almost thought that sleeping through the night would be better for him than food.

In the end, he couldn't bear to leave Walter alone.

He chivvied him up and out of the barn, practically ordering him to eat the apple and giving him the last of the water. They stumbled to the stream, but instead of jumping in to wash, they huddled together in the shadows, waiting for the elusive Emile.

Nate could no longer deny that Walter was sick.

The fear, the lack of food, lying in the stuffy, steaming barn covered in straw. All of it combined had sapped him, taken the core of steel and self-reliance that Nate had so admired in him. The man who was left leaned against Nate with a childlike trust, needing with a simplicity that chilled Nate to the bone.

Walter would not survive reassignment and deployment if he couldn't recover from losing his home in the woods of Moselle.

"Walter," Nate whispered, as he lay shivering against Nate's chest. "Walter, you must have hope. You will get better. The plane will get us, and you will find other soldiers to be your family too. And you and I will meet, when the war is over, in Times Square. I swear, I will wait for you. You are the only lover my heart can bear. You need to be strong for us."

Walter gave a sigh then and settled into a more comfortable position for sleep, and some of the ice in Nate's bowels relaxed. Sick, that was all. Of body, not of spirit. He would live. He would live, and their sad, faraway dream of life after the war could stay alive in their hearts.

This time, their contact arrived earlier, for which Nate was grateful. He left Walter asleep in the brush again and ventured out to meet Emile.

Emile turned out to be a sour, thin-faced man in his early twenties with a thick mustache and black hair hanging over his eyes. He wore a greasy beret that he positioned and repositioned as they spoke. It gave him a restless, fidgety air, and his sharp speech didn't endear him any further.

"So you are the great American," he snarled disagreeably.

Nate grunted. "I really am tired of hearing people say that," he said. "I am an American, and I am an officer in the USAAF, but beyond that, I'm a man who's spent the better part of a week hiding in a hayloft. It does not inspire greatness."

"It doesn't inspire trust, either. Where's your companion?"

"Sleeping in the brush," Nate said, wanting to hold his worry close. "I hope you have good news for us. He's ill and not getting any better."

"Oh, that's right, ill. That's why no one's seen him."

"What are you implying?" Nate snapped.

"I'm saying it's easier to get extra food if you claim to be an extra person!"

"Fuck your food!" Nate was taller than Emile, with a broader chest and apparently more righteous anger inside him. He pressed forward, watching with satisfaction as Emile stumbled backward, thumping up against a tree and huddling there, unable to escape. "Your help is appreciated, and the food too," Nate growled. "But I want to get back to my unit, and I want to get my film to intel, and I want to get Walter to safety. I *don't* want to play petty games. If there wasn't the chance that we could get out of here by plane, we would have left three days ago."

And maybe, wandering around the woods, they would have found a place, full of false promises and hope, but a place all the same.

"I just think it's damned convenient that you make such a big deal about your companion, and yet all we see of him is your need for us to put ourselves out for him, and Ouida's faint mention of a disagreeable little man—"

Nate turned away from him abruptly. "Is the plane coming or not?" he demanded.

"Tomorrow, midnight. Between the barn and the forest. It's flat enough for a landing strip, even for a small transport plane. Be waiting on the edges of the forest. Someone—Ouida or I—will be here to vouch for you or the pilot won't take you."

"We'll be here," Nate muttered, continuing on with his walk.

"Don't you want your food, American?" Emile taunted.

"Does it taste better than your offer of help?" Nate asked over his shoulder, and Emile let out a beleaguered sigh.

"I am sorry. Come. A man may get jealous, hearing about the mighty god who saved his woman."

Nate turned to him, sick in his stomach about relying on this irritating, jealous, weaselly little man for help. "I don't want your woman. All I want is to get my companion to safety. He lived in your woods for months, peacefully, until I crashed into his life, and then he gave all of that up to save me. He might still be there, happy, hiding beneath the floorboards while you deluded the Nazis, if not for me. And I have nothing to keep me here but him."

Emile dug into the satchel at his side and came up with a packet wrapped in linen, which he threw at Nate. Nate caught it midair.

"Be here," Emile sneered.

"If there is no plane, I'll paint an American flag on your door and call every Nazi for miles," Nate threatened baselessly. He didn't know where this man lived; all he knew of Moselle was the path from the woods to a farmer's barn.

"No need to get *nasty*," Emile said, his lip curling. "If your woman had been humping Nazis in the name of resistance, you'd be unpleasant too."

Oh, Father, spare him.

"She's worth ten of you," Nate said flatly. "And I'd rather spend this time in the barn." He turned his back on Emile then and faded into the shadows, carrying a loaf of bread and two more plump and rosy apples.

Walter was awake when Nate touched his shoulder, his eyes peering irritably into the dark. "He was a nasty piece of business. Makes me miss his girl."

Nate chuckled, hoping for some of Walter's laughter to wash away the bile. "And that could be the only time in your life you'll feel *that* way."

Walter smiled. "Did you get some food? I'll feel better if I eat."

Nate expelled a tension that had been weakening him for two days. "So will I."

They slept without reservation when they returned, and some of the peaceful glory of their first day in the barn returned with them. This afternoon, in the heated closeness, with the gold embers of dust floating from the skylight, Nate got to study Walter as he lay, eyes closed, Nate's hand on his thin chest.

His eyelashes were nearly transparent. It was a detail Nate hadn't really noticed before, because they had so few moments in the sun.

Walter's face, peaked, wan as it was, still lit from within, became glorious as Nate moved his hand from Walter's throat to the waistband of his trousers. As Nate cupped his manhood and stroked, Walter bit his lip softly, making it plump and red, and Nate scooted up, soothed the abused lip with the touch of his mouth, his lips, his tongue. He could feel Walter's heartbeat in the palm of his hand, with every stroke of his slender, pale cock. He barely remembered to fumble for the cloth to catch Walter's spend, but he did capture his gasp of climax deep in his mouth and swallowed it, held it close in his chest, and let it warm him with courage for the night to come.

They pulled apart, and Walter smiled at him, that same shy smile Nate had come to treasure. "We'll meet after the war," he said, voice ringing with conviction. "We have to."

They had to.

When the time came, Nate stopped at the door, his hand on the old-fashioned wrought iron latch. "A kiss for luck."

Walter's lips were sweet, but the kiss was too short. You cannot fit a lifetime into one meeting of lips, even if you try.

Two hours later, they crouched in the shadows at the fringe of the woods, scanning the sky. Walter was starting to shiver again, but Nate was hopeful. He could *hear* a plane, even if he couldn't see it yet. The low cloud cover hovered, rendering the landscape surrealistically bright in the kingdom of the nearly full moon.

The figure ghosting up next to Nate with feline grace was a familiar surprise.

"Ouida?" he asked unnecessarily.

"*Oui.* Emile was busy tonight. I said I would see you off."

Nate grimaced, not wanting to bear tales but unable to hide his dislike. "I'm surprised he wanted you alone with us. He seems to think I'm a threat."

"I am sorry," she whispered. "It was harder, I think, than he let on, seeing me with Horst. He has made threats against you. Our village is buzzing like a hornet's nest, and even knowing that I killed the Nazi and caused this mess has made his irritation worse."

"Be careful around him," Nate advised. He would walk away and leave this place, these people in chaos; the least he could do was tell her of his misgivings. "He is dangerous, and he is going to hold on to you with bony fingers. He may cut off your wrist to keep your hand."

"Is that a Yiddish saying?" she asked, sounding troubled.

"If it was, I would have said it in Yiddish," Nate replied mildly. Walter was crouched in the shadows next to the same tree Nate was leaning against, and his choked snicker gave Nate heart.

"I see he is feeling fit," Ouida observed dryly, and Nate tried to keep the misgiving from his voice.

"He will need a medic when we get back to the squadron," he said soberly. "He has a fever."

Ouida's expression—shown by the almost unnatural light—softened, and she patted Nate's shoulder. "Soon. Can you hear? There's the plane."

Nate peered out, and his optimism, which he'd only cautiously allowed to peek out at intervals during the day, suddenly gave a mighty leap.

They could *see* the plane now. It had dropped below the cloud cover, and the modified B-24 headed for the makeshift landing strip. Nate turned into the shadows and bent down to take Walter's hand, pulling him up.

"Come on, Walter. We are almost home free."

Walter grinned tiredly and stumbled out of the shadows, and then the sharp, echoing report of a handgun sounded, and he fell into Nate's arms.

"Walter?" His weight bore soddenly down, and the shots sounded again. Walter's body jumped in Nate's arms, and a terrible pain ripped through Nate. He fell backward, Walter's limp form on top of him, the hot slickness of blood coating Nate's arms, his chest, his heart.

"*Emile!*" Ouida's scream came from faraway, and the pain in Nate's body was screaming, screaming, and Walter wouldn't look up, wouldn't move, and they were both reeking in blood. The roar of the plane grew louder, louder than the shriek of Nate's heart, and Nate heard more shots, but closer, as Ouida, unwavering, killed her second lover in the span of a week.

Nate didn't care. The only man he would ever love wasn't breathing, wasn't moving. His head lolled back, showing glazed eyes and a gush of blood froth from his mouth.

Nate needed the blackness of unconsciousness, begged for it, prayed for it, so he wouldn't have to feel that grief with his whole heart.

Sometimes God is merciful. He never believed that with so much violence as he did the moment the world went black.

Walter, where are you? I can't feel you here. Shouldn't we both be dead together?

MOURNING FOR ONE, MOURNING FOR ALL

N ate wouldn't find out what happened to the film he'd carried until long after the war, but he was told that it was something important. Many of the OSS documents didn't become declassified until after the turn of the century, and by then, Nate was long past caring that a V-1 missile plant had been destroyed off the coast. It had been an important find tactically, and logistically, Captain Thompson's sacrifice and Walter's sacrifice had been well worth it to take those horrors out of play.

When Nate woke in the hospital in Menwith Hill, though, he was not feeling grateful for Walter's sacrifice. He was not particularly grateful to be alive, but that did not change either thing, and it didn't stop him from wishing himself dead.

The doctors told him repeatedly that he'd come close.

His second day of consciousness—after what amounted to three days of surgery and touch and go on his part—the woman who'd risked her life to fly in and pick him and Walter up came in with Ouida to tell the story.

They pulled up stools next to Nate's bed and sat in tense silence for a moment. The pilot was a plain-faced girl with a big smile and an unapologetically bold nose. Lieutenant Marion Mulder, whose husband was also a pilot in the war. In the coming days, she would visit him a lot, because she liked to talk and he was predisposed to listen. She would tell him stories about visiting her cousins in Brooklyn and Queens, and her favorite cousin, Carmen, who lived in Manhattan and was going to Vassar right now, but who would be graduating in a year or two and wanted to help in the war effort too.

But Nate knew none of that when both women first sat at his bedside. All he knew was that he wanted to die, and he was afraid to speak—not because he couldn't, but because all the recrimination and anger might come flooding out, and he would betray his and Walter's secret in a place where he might get a blue discharge at the very least for the things they had done in the cabin in Moselle.

"It was Emile," Ouida said baldly into the fraught silence. It took Nate a moment to register that she was using rusty English. "He was jealous. He wanted you dead for that."

"I figured that out." They were his first words in three days that hadn't been moans of pain or Walter's name.

"I'm so sorry." Ouida had aged in so short a time; her face thinner, the lines at the corner of her brown eyes deepening, her lips compressing, whether in bitterness or grief, he couldn't say. "I shot him, but it was too late. I think . . ." Nate knew what she was going to say, would have stopped her if he'd felt anywhere close to being able to control even the words in his mouth. "I think he was surprised when you pulled Walter out of the brush. He kept claiming that you were alone, you see. Nobody but you and I knew Walter existed. Emile didn't believe either of us."

"He believes us now," Nate said, surprised he even had room for irony.

"I suppose so," Ouida responded, some of the animation dying from her eyes.

More tense silence, interrupted by Marion. "Your friend, Walter?"

"Yes?" Nate glanced up quickly.

"He was already MIA, presumed dead—we looked into it while you were under. He doesn't have a next-of-kin listing. Is there any place you'd like him to be buried?"

Nate thought of their plans to live somewhere upstate, somewhere nobody knew them. And of his own aversion to cows and how Walter didn't seem to mind them at all.

"Albany," he said, thinking he could visit there as well as Long Island and that his parents were less likely to want to accompany him if he went. "The soldier's lot in Albany."

I can visit you there, Walter. It won't be like we planned it, but life seldom is.

"That'll be nice," Marion said. "You can visit on the weekends."

Nate felt laughter choke in his throat. It was so very what he had been thinking. He realized how long it had been since he'd been with his own people, someone who knew how far Albany was from Manhattan and would understand the Passover story, which he'd never had a chance to tell Walter. It comforted places in his heart that he didn't realize were raw.

"I am so sor—"

"Don't," Nate said, probably more gruffly than he intended. "Both of you. You worked very hard to help—so brave. I'm grateful. I'm just . . ." He couldn't even look at them. "Perhaps when I am healed, I will get a chance to fire a shot against the Nazis. Wouldn't that be nice? Perhaps I can be assigned to a fighting squadron instead of recon. Perhaps I can shed the blood, do the killing. I would like that, I think. I think I would like very much to have a red day, full of blood."

Father forgive him, he wanted somebody to pay.

He did not know it yet, because the doctors hadn't come to talk to him and, well, because the doctors still had hope, but that day would never come. Three bullets—fired through Walter's body—had shattered his femur and his pelvis. The bones had been wired back together, but one of Nate's legs—even after three more surgeries—would always be shorter, and his hip would give him pain until it was replaced near the turn of the century, when those things became common. By then, he would joke, he was so old he needed the cane anyway, but for a few brief years before the stroke, he could walk without pain, and that was a miracle.

But the miracle was in the distant future. In the near future, he would be sent to the Philippines to work with the OSS and Naval Intelligence and help interpret the photos that the other recon teams took. It seemed that, once they realized what he'd spotted from an airplane in the dark had been important enough to die for, they wanted to see what he could do with lots of magnification and decent lighting at his disposal. But he did not know that now. Now, he only knew that when his body healed, he could take his revenge and wreak all of the brutal, bloody havoc that seemed to fester from his heart.

In his whole life, he'd only once struck another person in anger—and that had been Walter. Now that Walter was gone, he wanted to murder until the seas ran red.

"I will help you," Ouida said fiercely, and he turned to her and felt his first moment of compassion since Walter had collapsed in his arms, so obviously dead that Nate hadn't needed to see his glassy eyes or the blood gushing through his mouth to know.

That hadn't stopped Nate from seeing those things in his anesthesia nightmares, from seeing Walter, sprawled next to him in the cargo hold of the plane while Ouida wept over Nate, trying to staunch the bleeding.

"I'd be honored," Nate said now, thinking of her fierceness with the gun, her unwavering destruction of her own lover in the face of betrayal. Brave girl. Her and Marion—brave girls. He turned his attention to Marion, suddenly remembering what a miracle it was that a plane had landed in occupied France.

"Your copilot . . .?"

"Is on a mission," Marion said, embarrassed. "I'm sort of grounded. You guys weren't exactly on our itinerary, but some crazy Mexican guy practically shoved me on the damned plane. His buddy—Irish kid, bad skin—pulled some *amazing* strings. The contact on the ground dropped your name, and they went insane. Said they knew you— you'd be the only guy on the ground there who'd drop his name to an OSS operative in the middle of France."

A terrible band of tension eased in Nate's chest. Walter was gone, yes, and Nate had left a gobbet of faith with his blood in the woods of Moselle, but he was not alone.

His face ached, and for a moment, he didn't recognize the feeling of a smile.

"Hector and Joey," he said. He was tired, falling asleep in fact, but it was fine.

Walter, we have people. We have friends. They put themselves out for us, Walter. Isn't that amazing?

"I can't wait to see them," he mumbled and then fell asleep.

They were there the next day, riotous, bitching, ribbing Nate about shirking his duty.

"All you had to do was take pictures!" Hector complained. "Pictures! What did you do?"

"Took the wrong pictures, I guess," Nate said through a tired smile. "The film was taken?"

"Yeah, we got it to intel," Joey said. "You probably don't remember, but Hector and I were there to meet the plane when it flew in. Didn't expect to find you shot up in the back. And *really* didn't expect the guy there with you to be an escaped POW from a dog's age ago."

"A surprise to us all," Nate said faintly, and the party atmosphere of the reunion sobered.

"And since we're all depressed anyway," Joey muttered, "they're gonna debrief you soon, but they want to know what happened to Captain Albert."

Nate grimaced. "Oy! Do you know that man died cursing me and kikes in general? He's lucky I went back to bury him."

Joey snickered. "That's . . . that's the meanest thing I've ever heard you say about *anyone*, Nate! That's *terrific!*"

"Good gravy, it's like he's a real soldier!" Hector chortled, and Nate grinned at them, conscious of the gap between his teeth and the way it made his smile look wicked for the first time in a month. Since he'd awakened on a couch in an abandoned summer home, talking nonsense to a little man who had frightened him with his self-sufficiency, he hadn't worried so much how others saw him. Walter had only known him for himself.

His grin faded though, and he remembered his words of blessing spoken over Thompson's body. "I left his insignia lodged in a tree in Moselle, where we interred the body. There should have been one dog tag in my pocket with the film and another is in the grave. When the war is over, he should be easy to find."

"You know, you're lucky your plane didn't break up during the crash. For all his faults, that man was a crack pilot." Hector nodded with the sage assessment of the expert. It stirred nothing in Nate's heart but respect for a friend, and he would remember that, because in later years, when he had cause to doubt, he *did* know what love was and how it was different than infatuation.

"Yes," Nate said, acknowledging. "And for that, I am, without reservations, grateful."

"Hey," Joey burst out. "You never did say—I mean, you ain't said nothin' really, cause we just got here and we been talking your ear off, but how did you meet that dead kid in the plane anyway?"

"He saved my life," Nate said. *You did, Walter. I don't know how I'm going to repay that, because I didn't return the favor.* "He dragged me out of the plane wreck and nursed me back to health."

Joey cackled, the shrill sound ringing across the tan tile and crisp white sheets of the hospital ward. "Well, too bad it wasn't that sweet French piece, right, Nate? Then you could have had a real adventure in the woods!"

"Since her boyfriend shot him up and he *didn't* get fresh with her, I think it's probably a good thing it was that other guy," Hector said practically. He smiled gently at Nate, patting his shoulder in a friendly way. "And I'm sorry about your friend, Nate. That's gotta be rough."

Nate tried to smile, but he couldn't anymore. Recovery, it seemed, was not nearly as much fun without Walter as it had been with him.

They left after that, but it was by no means their last visit. In fact, as the years passed, Hector and Joey became fixtures in his life. They moved in together after the war, roommates, bachelors. It was such a shame they never married.

Nate's children called them Uncle Joey and Uncle Hector, and if Carmen ever knew, ever suspected, she never batted an eyelash or so much as inflected a word. But then, Nate was never sure how much Carmen knew or guessed. He never wanted to know. They say women's hearts are secret gardens, but that is because men so rarely have anything to hide. Nate hid Walter in a little room in his heart for nearly seventy years. The garden in his heart where he visited his lover was lush and verdant by the time his favorite grandson took him out to listen for the bells of New Year's Eve, in a tradition that was the last reminder of a dead man and a month that no one alive remembered.

Nate's parents hadn't been informed that he was MIA or even wounded. Given that he was supposed to be taking pictures of officers, the brass had decided to keep his plane's disappearance a secret until it was known whether or not he'd survived. One of the first things he did during his recovery was to destroy the letter he'd written his parents.

He planned to write a new one, he did. But he could never figure out what he'd say. He'd start with the healing things, the growing things:

Dear Father—I'm sorry I left so angry. I realize now that although I may disagree with you on many things, I should never doubt that you love me. Mama, you and Father kept me alive and in plenty, fed rich in tradition, for lean, hard years. I can only give you my gratitude and return your love.

A promising beginning. He had several that began just like that. But as he wrote that part, the first part, he would find himself yearning to finish the letter:

I met someone, someone you would not approve of. I loved him in all the ways there is to love another human being. He died in the war, and a part of me died with him. I know you cannot forgive me for this, but you know me, and nobody knows him. I wanted him to live, in your minds if in no other way.

That was when he ripped up the letter into several pieces, kept the pieces under his pillow, and waited until the other patients were sleeping before he threw them away in the trash can being collected by the maintenance private to be sent to the incinerator.

What a laugh it would be if he got a blue discharge for a letter he never intended to send.

And then he discovered that he was no longer on active duty, and he had no reason for a letter. It was a load off his mind.

By the time he'd been transferred to HQ in the Philippines, he had resigned himself to a certain amount of emptiness, a certain amount of going through the motions. *Oh, Walter. Is this who I am without you? You would have been bored by me. I'm so sorry about that!* But emptiness didn't stop him from continuing with the war effort with his full heart. Terrible things—the farmer and his murdered cow small among them—were reported every day. Things so heinous that not even Nate believed them.

Marion's delivery route ran by Nate's location, and she looked in on him once or twice a month for that first year. Then came Normandy and the day when her copilot, Bess, actually flew the plane. Bess and

Nate practically carried Marion into Nate's quarters—he rated his own bunk as second lieutenant. She could not seem to stop crying.

Normandy took many, many young men, and her Ansel was one of them.

But the planes were stacking up, one after the other—so much intel, so many personnel, so many more places that needed information and weapons and men.

They gave her an hour—an hour to grieve a good man. It was a cheat, a cruelty, that's all it was. Nate and Bess had needed to carry her back to her plane, and one of the bravest things he'd ever seen was Marion wiping her swollen eyes, squaring her shoulders, and climbing up into the cockpit, her heart dead to the world.

For the first time since Walter, he had strength in him to pray.

Something must have worked. She was back two weeks later, with six hours' layover this time, which was enough for them to share dinner at the commissary and for him to pat her black armband awkwardly and give her proper condolences.

"Does it get better?" she asked, her voice broken. "Please tell me it gets better."

Suddenly, the wound he'd covered with activity and purpose, the belief that his life, his work in the war, was worthwhile, was wide open and bleeding again. And he wasn't sure he could even answer her honestly.

"I wouldn't know," he said tonelessly.

Her hand on his was the most human contact he could remember since Hector and Joey had embraced him before he'd been transferred to HQ.

"I'm going to take that as a no," she whispered. "I saw, Nate. I saw how you looked at him, the way you called his name. I'm not saying a nice girl wouldn't fix that, but for that moment, he meant something to you."

Nate closed his eyes. He had nowhere to run from this and nowhere to go to fix it. "Forever," he said. Then, in Yiddish, "*Alz*."

Marion squeezed his hand, and they sat in silence for a little while longer. Eventually she left, but, contrarily, that painful conversation gave him some hope. Marion would be well—he had no doubts. Maybe so would he.

So, for a minute, in the midst of war, he prayed for hope.

Until one day in August when he analyzed a piece of film from over Poland. It had been through two other spotters, each of whom had passed it on until it had landed on his table, where he crouched with his newly acquired tobacco habit and witnessed horrors from afar. It seemed Nate had an uncanny ability to read the story in the landmarks that made him great at this job. He thought it probably came from a lifetime of peering through a lens and trying to capture a story. *Wouldn't my father be surprised? He assumed these were silly children's tricks, and here they call me a magician.*

But he was not gloating that day in August of 1943 when he read the story of skeletons walking into a building from which there was no return.

He ran—or hobbled, but quickly—through the maze of the hastily thrown-up building in a place where the natives very smartly lived in bungalows with ceiling fans to combat the heat and the mosquitoes.

"Captain Perry!" he called breathlessly, bypassing the corporal acting his receptionist. "Captain Perry, did you know about this?"

The captain put down his phone and stared at the picture, listening to Nate's explanation of it with grim intent.

"Another one," he said flatly, closing his eyes. "Fuck."

Nate recoiled. "Another one? This isn't a concentration camp, Captain!" Because those had been bad enough. "Do you know what this is? The smoke here, the size of this room, the—"

It was too monstrous. Scarcely to be believed. How could this be on his desk, how could the world not know—

"Do you know what we can do about this?" the captain said bitterly, and Nate stopped ranting, desperate for hope.

"No."

"Can we bomb this thing?"

"No. We would destroy the people we are trying to protect."

"Can we stage a rescue operation?"

Nate knew how tight their personnel were, how many people would be used in an operation of only one camp. "For every concentration camp in occupied territory?" Auschwitz-Birkenau, Dachau, Chelmno, Bergen-Belsen—the list went on and on and on. Did they know which ones were doing this? Did they know if they were *all* doing it? This was a struggle of good and evil, and the terrifying thing was that they were so evenly matched. The Allies had *just* landed in Normandy, had *just* taken over France. Making their way through Germany and Poland to even get to these camps . . .

Nate's indignation quailed.

"There must be something we can do," he muttered in a small voice. "Oh, Holy Father, is there not *something*?"

Unlike Captain Thompson, this CO didn't give a damn if Nate was Jewish, Episcopalian, or—his own words—from some weirdo tree-hugging religion. He did his job competently and didn't piss off the people he worked with, and Perry had recommended Nate for the promotion to first lieutenant, which had meant Nate got a slightly bigger bunk and more filthy cigarettes to smoke. Nate was grateful the promotion didn't come with a transfer; he was good at his job here. He was, day by day, learning to survive with the hole in his soul. He didn't want to move if he could avoid it.

"There's only one thing we can do here to stop this," Perry said honestly. Nate knew what his answer would be before he said it. "Win this fucking war."

But winning the war didn't stop the horror of it, the betrayal via the inaction of what Nate had once thought of as a defending country and a loving God.

And the only thing that stopped the horror was more horror.

PICTURES IN
BLACK AND WHITE

B y the time Nate was discharged, sent back to his parents' home in Manhattan with commendations and a purple heart and a sheaf of papers from the Pentagon with his signature promising to talk about perhaps only ten percent of what he had done in the war, his inner monologue with Walter was a constant thing. Inside his head and his heart, his garden was green, and there were flowers of memory—a poppy-colored kiss, lemon sunshine in a smile, the purple of a passionate night, the forbidden gold of a day in the sun.

Outside his head and his heart, the world was gray, black, and white, like a movie but without sound, without dialogue, without laughter or movement.

He embraced his father when he walked off the plane, and the absent tenderness that coated his icy heart was the first thing to warm him since he'd been asked to analyze some of the first aerial photos of Japan.

"You were wounded?" his father asked jovially, seeing the cane and the weight loss and the nicotine stains on the fingers of his son who had never smoked until hours spent over a photo table. "How is it you were wounded when all you did was take pictures of the officers and their wives?"

Nate had no room inside him for jokes, even ones made hopefully, in the interest of keeping peace. "Papa, the whole world was wounded. We're still bleeding."

Selig Meyer was, like Nate, a large man, and his face had grown broader with age. For the first time, though, Nate saw the flesh of him droop and sag, grow old. "I know, Nathan. I had just hoped better for my one remaining son."

If Nate had any doubts then that Walter had been right, and that his father's parting had sprung from anything *besides* embarrassed love, they died a quiet death. His heart thawed just a trifle more, and he hugged Selig again. They might never reach a perfect understanding—fathers and sons didn't always, particularly not the children of war and depression. But Nate raised his children with the sure knowledge that his father loved him and that he needed to do a better job of showing them the same thing.

Nate's mother had no such reservations.

"You are too thin. Let's get you home, and you can get back your strength." She glared at him, unafraid. "And no smoking in the house. It's a terrible habit. You smell like an ashtray."

She'd begun to dye her hair black since he'd left for the war, and her coiffure and composure were, as always, impeccable, right down to the perfectly applied red lipstick that suited her. But her eyes—large, brown, and expressive, like his—were lined at the corners and worried. Nate remembered Walter telling him that he'd quit smoking on the POW train because nobody had cigarettes, and how neither of them had cared enough about the habit to take Captain Albert's stash under his seat.

It would be nice to reclaim that man again, even in so small a matter as cigarettes, so Nate used his mother's strictures as an excuse to cut down and then to quit. Of course, as years passed and the world realized what a tremendous matter cigarettes really were, Nate had cause to think that Walter had, once again, saved his life, even in death. It seemed that the habit of watching after Nate was too great for even bullets to stop.

"Yes, Mama," he said dutifully, and for a moment, he had cause to think the frost surrounding his heart would thaw, that he could remember what it was to live again.

But it was not that easy.

When he'd been stationed at HQ, he'd slept like the dead, because death was what he woke up to every day. When he slept at his parents' house, he woke up to the living, and every morning when he heard his mother in the kitchen and his father calling him down for breakfast, he thought one of two things.

Sometimes it was that he was a child and his brother Zev had let him sleep in.

More often, he was in Moselle, and Walter was doing battle with the wood stove to cook him breakfast.

And then the reality would sink in, and he'd be alone in the room he'd left when he went away to college, and the griefs, both of them, would weigh down the lightness of waking with the heaviness of sleep eternal.

He arrived home in August of 1946. In October, he began his once-weekly trips—a train and three buses—to the cemetery in Albany. The grave site was pristine. He stretched out his wounded leg and hip doing the small bit of gardening required to keep it that way. He had to cut down his visits when the weather became severe, but he went four of the eight days of Chanukah. He stood in the snow and told Walter about the traditions—the miracle of the oil that burned for eight days, the games with the dreidel, and the coins made of chocolate. It seemed silly, perhaps, standing in the cold and preparing a dead man for what amounted to his bar mitzvah, but it felt very necessary to Nate.

You need to be ready, Walter. When I join you, I'm going to expect you to know all sorts of things, so we can stroll about Gan Eden together, and you will be prepared.

Even the most wicked of men only went to the other place for what amounted to less than a year. Walter was far from the most wicked of men; he would be waiting for Nate when Nate had spent his time in Gehinnom.

Nate had much to atone for, living being chief among his sins.

Six million Jews. Six million. It was . . . The number was . . . Seventeen million people? Six million Jews? Who wakes up one morning and decides to simply *annihilate* part of the world's population, like cutting away fabric?

The atomic bomb. It vaporized people. Left nothing more than shadows etched into the stone and sickness and horror afterward. Nate had seen the pictures, had read the stories, had felt his heart shrink and quail at the suffering.

Like the world, when the first euphoria of the war ending faded, Nate spent much of his time simply reeling from these facts, closing in on himself, afraid, because any thought past eating and helping his father in the shop hurt. There were demons. There were monsters. They lurked outside the door, and in the newspapers and magazines, and in the eyes of the returning veterans, and in the hearts of the bitter, angry, despondent people who over and over again asked, *Why?*

It was a time when Jews gathered together, afraid of additional hostility, comforting each other in their communal grief, and Nate, ever the outsider, could not do that.

He tried to go to temple during Yom Kippur, because every Jew in the city spent his day in temple—it was the day of atonement.

But he couldn't sit through prayers, and midway through the first service, he turned from his place in the back of the small temple, just blocks from his parents' house, and made his way through the crowd lamenting the things they'd allowed to happen because they hadn't known.

He was stopped by one of the younger rabbis, a man who'd gone on to lead the church into Reformed Judaism, one of the freer thinkers who believed in atonement and that intentions mattered more than laws.

"Nathan," he chided, reminding Nate that he'd only been a few years older than him as they were coming up through school. "You cannot even sit through prayers?"

Nate regarded him bleakly.

"Rabbi, you must regret the sins you ask to atone for," he said, thinking painfully of Walter's head resting against his chest. "I . . ." He turned away. "I can't."

"Then perhaps they weren't sins," Rabbi Oskar said tentatively, and Nate closed his eyes.

"And perhaps they were, and I am simply the Wicked." He said it, trying to make a joke, but his voice fell, and it sounded very, very real.

The rabbi's hand on his sleeve was gentle. "And perhaps you were just the Young," he said hopefully.

Nate shook his head. "I shall never be young again," he said, meaning it.

And he walked away that day, thinking about Walter and how he'd never regret that sin, and couldn't atone for what hadn't felt like a sin at all. And that the biggest sin, the sin of seeing what the world was doing to his people and being locked into inaction, was something his country would not allow him to tell.

So he mourned for the world, and he mourned for one man, and his grief for the one man set him apart from the world.

New Year's Eve, 1946, was unbearable. When had his plane been shot down? 1943 He'd lived nearly five years after that? It was unthinkable. He had to have something to look forward to.

It was that thought that drove him outdoors, walking from his parents' brownstone to Times Square. Nearly a thirty block walk in the cold—he would move closer in future years, when his business took off—and he was making it in a thin coat with a cane. The twinges in his hip and his thigh were agonizing, but in a way, the pain was a blessing. When he was in pain, at least he could see red.

Times Square was manic, even in those days before the place was lit up like daylight and the bleachers were put in. He made it within two blocks, though, and found a building to lean against, closing his eyes against the chill of the granite against his back.

I'm here, Walter. I'm here, and I'm listening. Will they ring for us, do you think? My God, Walter, I need to hear them. I need to hear some beauty in the world or I will fade away from it, like a photograph that never developed.

He shed bitter, bitter tears then, his shoulders heaving, gasps tearing from his throat, heedless of the stares of passersby.

He would need to take a bus home, eventually, and he was chilled so badly, he had to stay in bed with a fever for the next week. It wasn't until he was lying in bed with his face toward the wall, his mother's matzo ball soup cooling on his bed stand, that he realized he felt strangely lighter.

He remembered waking up in Menwith Hill and how terrible a secret he was hiding with Walter's death, and realized: he had borne, and he had mourned, but he had never cried.

He had needed to cry.

At the end of his convalescence that week, he got a welcome surprise. Marion knocked on his door, her black armband gone and a new wedding ring in its place.

At her side was her cousin, Carmen, the one who'd been going to Vassar.

The two women came bustling into his bedroom, where he was sitting up in his pajamas, reading a newspaper. His father's business was doing very well, but Nate was hoping to find a studio. Perhaps, if he were to start taking pictures again, he thought restively. Perhaps . . .

He looked up at the two of them, a polite smile on his face.

"Your mother seems to think you're at death's door," Marion said practically. "You seem healthy enough to me. Shirking your duty, that's what you're doin'!"

And that elicited a warm grin. "Well, the military gave us no time to shirk, so I'm doing it all now! How are you? Happy, I hope."

Marion nodded and proceeded to regale Nate and her cousin with the story of how she met her Saul and how it would be true love forever. It probably was true love forever, but she lived to bury Saul, and Ephraim after him. Ezra—fifteen years her junior, and very much in love—had been the one to bury her, when she'd passed away late into her eighties. But now, in this moment, she was a friend, and one who made him smile, and he so badly needed to smile.

Her cousin didn't say much that day, just listened to Marion with a smile and laughed in all of the appropriate places. When they stood to leave, she took his hand.

"I hope you feel better." Her smile was perfect, with even, white teeth, and her blonde hair peeked out from under the little cap on her head. The man in him didn't notice these things, but the photographer in him awoke, wishing for the Kodachrome slide film to capture the contrast between her blonde hair and her red lips.

He knew what would make a pleasing picture. But the pleasing picture of a woman did not stir him.

Still, her appearance—and that desire for a picture—made enough of an impression that he bought a camera and some film.

The first thing he took a picture of was Walter's grave.

Morbid, of course. But he had no pictures of Walter, no mementos. The doll that he'd carried in their flight through the forest had been shattered when Nate had fallen with Walter on top of him. Nate had nothing but that grave site to prove it had ever happened.

He took the picture in the spring, before Passover, when crocuses and daffodils and lilies were everywhere. Nate left a bouquet of them on the grave, making sure no other visitors there could see, and then pulled out his Leica and . . .

And composed a picture. Light, shadow, form, line—he remembered these things. He had a degree in art and history—if a man didn't paint, this was the thing, perhaps, to do with it.

He began to take his camera everywhere in the city to photograph the usual things: The Empire State Building, the skyline at night. The streets from the rooftops, and from the pavement, the sky. His black-and-white photos from that time were some of his best work . . . and his most private. He saw Carmen often in the city during his rambles with his camera: in the library, in the museum where she worked, on her way to temple. Often, he nodded and waved, speaking pleasantly to her. Occasionally he bought her a cup of coffee or a bagel at a kiosk, and they caught up on the news from Marion, who was living with her new husband in New Jersey and still visited.

But for all that they saw each other in passing, he never in that time took her picture, never celebrated the color of her hair or the glint of her smile in Kodachrome. All he saw, all he photographed, was the black and the white. It meant his eye was not distracted by color, and he could compose the picture with only line and shadow in mind.

He told her that once, about the black and white, but he never let her see the pictures he took. He assumed she forgot about them. Even after Carmen's death, he kept them up in his room, under his bed, and he'd given copies of them to only three people, none of whom would betray his secret for the world. Most of the photos—by trick of light, by accident of shadow or line—were shockingly masculine and astonishingly sexual, not that there were any male models to make them that way. Most of the time, he hadn't been conscious of taking a picture that suggested a man's back, or his phallus, or the length of his flank, but that was the picture he would develop in the little darkroom in the back of his father's shop.

He loved those pictures. Sometimes when he was working on them, he would array them in the darkroom, as though he were at a gallery showing, and trace the lines that reminded him of Walter, finding the corrugation of his ribs in a bicycle rack and the poetry of his shoulder blade in the silhouette of a car on the pavement.

They were the best work he'd ever done.

But although they sustained him for that spring and summer, by the time fall came, he was fighting his way, day by day, through melancholy, and he had no heart for those pictures in October of 1947. He had visited Walter's grave the day before, a chilly Friday evening laced with the fluttering of falling leaves, like bat's wings, and came to some sort of decision. He must move forward or die. He could not leave Walter behind entirely, but his picture-taking could no longer be the kind to feed his soul. He would have to make it into a livelihood.

Thus, he sat in the library, researching how to apply for a business permit and what items he would need for a photographic studio of his own.

He had money—and the government would help subsidize a business of his, as a veteran—but somehow, even investing in the paperwork felt like a betrayal.

Silly, wasn't it? How moving on from a life you never had was still a denial that you might ever have it?

So that left him where? Mourning in his childhood room? Never leaving his father's shop? And because why? Because he was afraid Walter wouldn't be able to find him?

Walter wasn't going anywhere. And at this rate, neither was Nate.

"You look as though you're losing an argument with yourself."

Nate glanced up, startled, and he had to focus his eyes to recognize the pretty girl Marion had brought to his bedside in January and whom he'd seen periodically since.

"I am," he said, attempting to smile so she wouldn't worry. "I am trying to decide if I want to set my business in Manhattan or Queens."

She grimaced. "Manhattan, of course," she said, nodding. "Because my parents live in Queens, and this would give me the excuse to get out of Queens and come visit."

He smiled. "There's a certain hubris there," he said, making sure she understood. "If a business fails in Queens, well, you start another business. If a business fails in Manhattan . . ."

"You end up working for somebody else," she said, nodding soberly. Only her dancing eyes let him know she was taking this as play.

"Or you try again in Queens," he said, and she laughed. She had a nice laugh, he thought, remembering those coffees, the hurried chats on the steps in front of the museum, and the times he'd done little more than tip his hat in passing.

All of which reminded him—

"No," she said, when he started to pack up his books and set them aside to shelve. "We were having such a lovely time. Don't run away from me, Mr. Meyer. I was just settling down for a good talk."

And a part of him really wanted to. And a part of him was lonely, so lonely and so tired of grief in its many forms.

He settled back down with a forced smile. "Well then, a talk with a pretty girl. How can a man resist?" Well, a man such as Nate, he could. But he didn't, not this time.

And not when Carmen followed him home, still talking, angling for an invitation to dinner that his mother readily gave.

Walter wasn't going anywhere, and no other man was worth the isolation. The pictures were just that—flat and stark and full of mourning. At least with Carmen, there was laughter, a certain quickness, a feisty sense of humor. This girl would be a partner, not a burden.

And Walter had taught him all about partnership, so Nate would know.

So he didn't resist, not through invitations to dinner, not through invitations to the movies.

Not through that first night when Carmen, hesitatingly and giggling through her blushes, invited him to stay at her apartment for coffee.

She'd had another lover before him—for all he knew, a score of them, but she was a sweet girl, shy when they were undressed, gentle of touch, so he assumed one or two at the most. She assumed he'd had others, and he never, not in nearly sixty years, ever disabused her of that notion.

They trembled together that first night, and snuck glances from under lowered brows. He asked her, in a polite whisper, repeatedly, what felt good, and he was willing to give her directions of his own.

It didn't move the world—not his world, anyway—but when it was over, she lay with her head on his shoulder and looked at him worshipfully. In the light from the streetlamp, he could see the gleam of her hair and the blue of her eyes, and thought once again of colored film.

That New Year's Eve, she asked to go with him, and he refused.

"I'm sorry," he said, awkward with her for the first time since they'd started having sex. "This thing I do is very personal to me. I would prefer to be there alone."

She seemed to acquiesce, but Carmen had stubborn moments.

He was not aware she had followed him until he stood, in the same corner, eyes closed, listening for bells that wouldn't ring.

It was his grieving time.

Walter, she's beautiful, not that you would care. But her soul is beautiful too. She is funny, and she argues with me in the fun way, and mein Gott, tateleh, my heart is just so lonely without you. And I'm sorry, but I need my people if I can't have you. I need to go to temple and know the traditions. I need to gather with them and grieve at the terrible, terrible thing they survived. Please, Walter, I just need to know—

"Nathan?" Her voice snapped him from his reverie, from the place and the time when he felt closest to Walter, and he didn't remember what he said to her, but it was angry and mean—when Nate was never mean.

He finished with, "Go to hell, you stupid girl! I don't need you, and I don't want you in my life!"

He had moved to an apartment in December, so she didn't have to endure the glares of her landlady and so he could feel like an adult in the world, and the next morning, she was at his door.

She looked pitiful and bedraggled, and carried with her steaming bagels for breakfast and a small carton of fresh juice.

He had tossed on his bed that night, unable to sleep after being deprived of his conversation with Walter, and ashamed of his anger, but she didn't ask for an apology.

"Here," she said, handing him the bagel. "I know you didn't eat. Please let me in. I have something to say."

He nodded, and she walked purposefully into the studio apartment. He'd counted. Two steps to the table, three steps to the couch, five steps to the bed in the corner. If you walked into the bathroom and out again, it was ten steps total—he was sure prisons had bigger cells.

She'd spent an entire night when she had work the next morning sewing him curtains for his one window in the bathroom.

"The bagel is nice," he said when they were seated at the table with breakfast. "Thank you."

She nodded, chewing thoughtfully, then swallowed and sighed.

"I love you, Nathan. I look at our elders, the immigrants who survived the war, and I see plenty of people huddling together for comfort, but none of them for love. But I love you. And I think you love me. Now you didn't ask our first night together, but you knew I wasn't a virgin, and you didn't judge and I thought that was nice. And Marion told me you were grieving for someone during the war. So here's the thing: I can give you New Year's Eve. I can. Whatever prayers you were saying for her, I can give them to you. But you got to give me everything else. I'll let you go to Albany four times a year, and I promise not to go see who's buried there, and you can go say your prayers on New Year's Eve. But that's all she gets. Can you live with that? Can you live with me?"

Carmen's voice, which was Vassar by way of Queens, had hardened for a minute, no-nonsense, and her parents' accents slipped through. But her hard tones crumbled, and her lower lip wobbled, and that surprising vulnerability—much like Walter's—peeped through.

He took her hands. "I was asking permission," he said, which was as much of the truth as he ever told her about this matter. "I was asking permission to be with you."

Carmen nodded, pulling one hand away to wipe her face with the back of it. She'd worn no makeup this day, and her nose and eyes were puffy already from tears.

"Did you get it?" she asked, sounding like a child. *Ah God. Walter, I can't let her be hurt any more than I could with you.*

But he couldn't lead her on about his intentions, either. "I would need to be buried in Albany," he said, feeling awful. She recoiled as though shot.

"Nate, that's not even a Jewish cemetery!"

"No," he agreed evenly, looking her full in the eyes. Carmen was anything but *frum*, but that didn't mean she didn't go to temple with her parents, and it didn't mean she didn't believe that being buried in a Jewish cemetery was integral to having a Jewish afterlife. So now she knew. If they married, it was for life, but not for death. His family, his faith, they could have him now, because he couldn't make it alone. But he'd promised Walter they could be together. This was how.

She was going to say no, he thought, almost relieved, but then she nodded, wiped her eyes. "Maybe you'll change your mind," she said after a moment, and he opened his mouth to end it right there. "Maybe not," she finished, reminding him very much of his own mother, negotiating with the butcher. "But if you don't, that's your loss. I'll be spending the afterlife with family, our children, our parents. You'll be spending it in Albany." She sniffled, truly upset, but then she met his gaze defiantly, and for the first time since the war, he felt of worth. "I can make that bargain."

Her voice broke, and she began to cry.

He pulled her against his chest and grabbed a paper napkin from their breakfast. She snuggled in, and although she didn't quite fit, was too soft in some places and too bright in others, he took her anyway.

"I doubt you'll be lonely," he said. "Should we invite Marion to the wedding?"

They did, and they invited Hector and Joey, and Ouida, as well.

The night before the ceremony, which would be a modest one, with Carmen's hand-embroidered *chuppa* as the only real bit of finery, Carmen went out with her friends for a "hen party" (Marion's words). Nate hoped Carmen didn't begrudge him his own friends from the war.

The four of them went out drinking the night before the ceremony, and Nate brought with him two of three packages—flat, taped together, cardboard, labeled *Do not bend* on both sides. The third of the three would live under his bed for the rest of his life, moving with him from apartment to brownstone, never to be opened.

Ouida spoke passable English and lived in New Jersey now and was one of the few women at the bar they chose. Nate, who had seen her shoot two lovers in the same week, did not marvel that she could frighten away any interloper with a sneer and a curl to her red lip. She seemed determined not to allow anyone to interrupt their celebration.

Although, as the bartender set down their second round of drinks, it was grimly apparent that nobody at the table felt like they were celebrating.

"So Nate," Hector said, matter-of-fact, downing his Scotch with practice. He'd been going to college for the past two years, and he no longer resembled the young dockworker who would cut a rug in his zoot suit. Such a shame—Nate had been a little in love with that man.

"Yes," Nate said, his usual quiet smile in place.

"This girl . . . I got to say, Joey and me, we're pretty surprised it's a girl."

Nate swallowed, hard. He thought they might have been.

"Me as well," he admitted, and he tried to evade Ouida's perceptive glance as he stared at his own Scotch.

"You cannot compromise with your lovers," Ouida said. "You can't sleep with someone because of what they can give you, as opposed to what you should be giving them."

Nate grimaced. Well, Ouida would know. "Guys," he said, peering sideways at Joey and Hector. Well, if they weren't as he suspected, would they even know what they were looking at?

He pulled out his packages and gave one to Hector and one to Ouida. "These . . ." He sighed. "These are parts of me I'm giving up, marrying Carmen. I need you to keep them safe." He watched Joey snatch the package from Hector and then dig into it with eager fingers. Nate reached out and smacked Joey's hand.

"If you value . . . *anything*, you won't open those here," he said, and Joey stopped, an expression of comic dismay crossing his face.

Hector turned to his roommate and patted his cheek, and that was when Nate saw it: tenderness. There was tenderness in that gesture—not the brisk kidding of buddies, but gentleness, a certain affectionate understanding.

Nate knew then that his guess had been completely on target, and these men, who had shared his bunk back at Menwith Hill, were now sharing something completely different together.

He figured the pictures would be the closest thing to a wedding present he'd ever give them.

"Oh," Joey said now, embarrassed. Then, being Joey, and having a heart as big as the world: "We'll keep your heart safe for you, okay, Nate? Promise. You make Carmen happy; we'll keep this part secret."

Nate picked up his drink and held it aloft, nodding at each of his friends in turn. "To Walter," he said softly, one of the few times his name would be said aloud from that moment on.

"To Walter," they said, all of them with reverence.

They clinked glasses and drank.

Nate and Carmen were married the next day.

THE SUN SETS

Fifty-nine years together—not bad, really. They'd been good years, mostly. Nate had his four trips a year to Albany and his one night at New Year's, listening for bells that would have stopped tolling in 1945, if they ever had rung.

He didn't tell Carmen about his almost-daily conversations with his dead lover. He kept Walter apprised of his children and his business, then his grandchildren, then his retirement. He told him about Hector and Joey, and how they passed away within a week of each other, and how their relatives were scandalized to discover that there was only one bed in their two-bedroom apartment and a series of decidedly uncomfortable photographs on the walls of the empty room, which they used as a library. He mentioned Ouida, who married one man and loved him until she died of lung cancer in the late eighties.

When Carmen passed away, Nate had been lost and sad. She'd been his best friend, his confidante in everything but Walter, and he'd missed her. He'd taken many portraits of her and their family as time had progressed, though. The Carmen of his memory was a grandmother, with a full life under her belt. The Walter he still loved was as young and as full of potential as Nate was, the unlived part of him, the part that lay boxed up under his bed in the black-and-white photos that his family would probably find at his death and wonder at.

But young or not, he was sure Walter had been trying to comfort him for the past six years since she'd gone. He'd told Walter that the hard thing was the thought that they wouldn't meet in the afterlife, even to be friends. But then, she would have her family and her parents, and Nate's family and parents. Nate would be content to have Walter in the afterlife, as he would have been to have Walter, and Walter only, in life. So in those years was a reconciling. Nate would have Walter, and Carmen would be surrounded by love. It was not everything, but it was all he could do.

This year he'd had the stroke.

And a certain amount of relief had dawned on him. All this time, dedicated to keeping Walter a secret in his heart, and now there was no way he wouldn't be. Walter was his, and no one could take that away.

Nate sat, swathed in his heaviest coat and a leather hat with a lamb's wool lining, and listened for the bells.

Blaine shook his shoulder slightly, trying to get his attention.

"You understand, don't you, *Zayde*?" he asked anxiously, and Nate didn't have to remember.

Of course I understand. Of course I do. I want this boy for you. I want your happiness. I want you to have all the things I did not, the things I kept secret from the world.

"It's just that I love him." Blaine's voice grew thick, and Nate damned his inability to pat his grandson's cheek. "I love him so much. And I didn't even know, I didn't even say the word *gay* in my head. But Tony—I mean, you've met him, *Zayde*. He's something. He's so proud. And I want to be like him, right? Proud and brave. You understand that, don't you?"

I'm so proud of you. You're so brave. Isn't he brave, Walter? Don't you think he's amazing?

Yeah, Nate. He's just like you.

Walter? Nate turned his head then, and there he was. He wore a camel coat with a little snap-brim news cap and had a tweed suit on under the coat. His eyes were that amazing turquoise that Nate hadn't seen since.

You didn't want the fedora? Nate asked, puzzled.

Walter shrugged and smiled shyly. *I haven't grown into it yet*, he apologized. *Maybe after a few years of us together, I'll be big enough for the fedora.*

Nate smiled at him, feeling tears behind his eyes. *It's your hat,* tateleh. *Heaven forbid you not wear the one you want.*

Walter looked away wistfully, toward the sound of the revelers many blocks away. *Have you heard them yet, Nate? The bells that ring for both of us? Because as much as I appreciated the dreidels on my grave site, I wouldn't mind hearing the church bells.*

No, Walter. My God, it's good to see you. Nate wanted to get up and embrace him, but Blaine was asking him something first.

"You understand, right, *Zayde*?"

Poor boy. He sounded desperate, and Nate wanted to give him something, anything, before he went to hold Walter. It had been so long. He pushed and pulled at his lungs, at the muscles in his face, thinking *I can do this, I can tell him!* when suddenly, he heard them, the vibrations pulsing through the soles of his feet and up into the soul of his body.

Nate? Nate! Do you hear—

I hear them, I hear them! You were right! They're ringing! I hear them.

Oh no! He needed to kiss Walter, right now, before the bells stopped. They had no traditions, not even a picture; they needed to do this.

But he couldn't just leave Blaine, either.

"*Zayde*?" A sound of upset, of sadness in Blaine's voice. Well, Nate couldn't help that. This new generation had so many of the things Nate's generation had fought for. Blaine could have this, Nate was sure of it.

"*Alz*," he said, forcing the word with everything in his body. He smiled with all of his face when it should have been impossible and patted Blaine's hand with his weak hand, as it grasped the strong one. "God give you *alz*." All family, here and in the afterlife, so Blaine would not have to make the choice Nate had made years ago and was about to carry through.

Blaine turned shining eyes toward him, and Nate's eyes closed. In a breath, then two, he was free of his body altogether. Strong and hale, he stood and stepped around Blaine to haul Walter into his arms. He smelled good—healthy—of milled soap and aftershave, and Nate buried his nose in those clean, orange curls and breathed again.

The church bells were chiming loud enough to drown out Blaine's sobs. Tony was running down the block, the coffee in his hands, and

Nate forgot about them, because they had their own life to live. Nate didn't any longer. He had Walter, warm and willing, stubble rasping Nate's cheeks as they tasted each other, devoured each other, held each other's faces and kissed like starving men, feeding from the other's soul. The kiss ended, and he pulled back, the heat from Walter's body seeping through this frigid January morning, making him smile.

"Took you long enough," Walter said, grinning to show he wasn't mad.

"I missed you so badly," Nate told him, closing his eyes against tears. *No tears now.* He finally had everything he wanted. He had *alz*.

But Walter's lips were salty too, and Nate opened his mouth to his kiss, and the part of his heart he'd thought was dead, the part buried under the bed in black-and-white photos, was now alive, in breathing color. Around them, through their awakening senses, the sound of the long-awaited church bells baptized them with the sound of hope.

AUTHOR'S NOTE

My grandparents were spies in the war.

I've said this more than once, both on my blog and in person, but I've always thought it's an amazing thing. My children read about the war in history books and I get to tell them, "Your great-grandmother and great-grandfather both served in the OSS in WWII!"

And it sounds *great*!

But it's also a little ambiguous.

My grandfather wrote two adventure stories based on his time with the OSS—but neither of them gave a whole lot of detail about what he actually *did*. In one story, he was flying from Europe to America or the Philippines with a plane full of photographs to be analyzed when he was shot down over Greece. He was rescued by fishermen who stole his wallet (I swear, this is the story he told on the DVD that the Living History people recorded) and lived for six months in Greece, covertly helping the Greek resistance. During that time, he delivered a baby next to the SS Headquarters on the island, and was hidden in a wheat bin when the officers came to ask what the ruckus was.

I mean, how could you *not* think that's brilliant and amazing?

The real question, of course, is whether or not it's true.

Given how many times Grandpa put that story into print or told the story on film, I'm thinking it was the truth—or at least part of the truth. Grandpa certainly worked for the OSS in both WWII and Korea, and he was definitely declared MIA during WWII. He used a code name, because when he and Grandma met, he told her that his name was Phillip, and her family was *very* confused when after the war, she married Kenneth instead. But when I was researching this very book, I saw a list of the OSS officers who were sent in to help reclaim Greece from the Axis during a very tricky political/military maneuver, and I saw the name "Alex Phillips." You may wonder what this has to do with anything—*but . . .*

But seeing that Grandpa named his one son Phillip (and one of his daughters Monica Phil), it's apparent he has a habit of naming his offspring after his code names.

And my mother's name is Alexa Ken.

So you can see my skepticism with some of the cover story for why he was in Greece—but I don't doubt that he was there, and given that he made his living after the war as a documentary filmmaker, I don't doubt that he was a photographer during the war. So, in his honor, when I wanted a character who flew missions, I didn't make that character a fighter pilot; I made him a photographer, and then I went about looking up how that photographer would take pictures from miles up in the air.

In some cases, the photography was automated. In some cases, special equipment was needed, and so the pilot would have been assigned to transport a photographer. I assumed that Grandpa would be in the latter situation, since he'd never touted his skills as a pilot, and, as far as I know, of the four plane crashes he lived through (four!), he was not flying during any one of them.

But I don't know for certain.

Just like when Grandma told me that she was in the office of dirty tricks, and then actually recounted what some of the tricks *were*, I have no idea of knowing how much of that was true and how much was Grandma, who loved a good story. Was her tale of using covert radio lines to tell POWs to sabotage their captors before Allied attacks real, or did she watch *Hogan's Heroes* and like that story better than what she actually did accomplish during the war? (Given that she had me believing that a story straight from *The Godfather* was actually a part of her childhood, I do have the right to be a little skeptical.)

Again, I do not know—not for certain.

But I know she worked for the OSS, and I know that her work was only recently declassified, and I know that in civilian life, she was a gutsy, determined, creative woman, so I will choose to believe that her stories were true.

And speaking of stories that might be true: one night, as I was stumbling through the internet on autopilot, I ran across a story about how a certain church in New York chimed its bells on New Year's Eve when the soldiers were away at war. I read the article, was inspired by it, and then lost it—*literally* could find no trace of it again.

So I shall do what I have practice doing—choose to believe it was true.

And I will choose to believe that WWII was one of the last unambiguous times in our world's history, where there was, for all intents and purposes, a clear good and a clear evil.

And I will choose to believe that we didn't learn nearly enough from that horrible destruction of life, and that the state of our world now is proof.

So when I think about Grandma and Grandpa being spies in the war (as my aunts and uncle and I tell ourselves), I also think about how they left a better world for us, but like Nate's grandson, it is our job to take that better world and to continue to move it into the future.

Thanks to my grandparents, I'll keep hope that we can do just that.

Dear Reader,

Thank you for reading Amy Lane's *The Bells of Times Square*!

We know your time is precious and you have many, many entertainment options, so it means a lot that you've chosen to spend your time reading. We really hope you enjoyed it.

We'd be honored if you'd consider posting a review—good or bad—on sites like **Amazon, Barnes & Noble, Kobo, Goodreads, Twitter, Facebook, Tumblr,** and your blog or website. We'd also be honored if you told your friends and family about this book. Word of mouth is a book's lifeblood!

For more information on upcoming releases, author interviews, blog tours, contests, giveaways, and more, please sign up for our weekly, spam-free newsletter and visit us around the web:

Newsletter: tinyurl.com/RiptideSignup
Twitter: twitter.com/RiptideBooks
Facebook: facebook.com/RiptidePublishing
Goodreads: tinyurl.com/RiptideOnGoodreads
Tumblr: riptidepublishing.tumblr.com

Thank you so much for Reading the Rainbow!

RiptidePublishing.com

ACKNOWLEDGMENTS

I'd like to thank Del Kostka for answering my questions after I read his online article, Damon Suede for giving me a few brief lessons on Jewish history in New York, Jay from Joyfully Jay, who helped me not offend anybody, and Gloria, who told me that Nate's voice in her head reminded me of her grandparents, which I took to be an amazing compliment.

And Sarah and Rachel, of course, who said, "Tragic gay holiday story? Of *course* we'll publish that!"

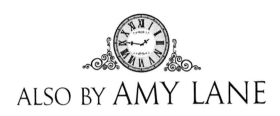

ALSO BY AMY LANE

For a complete booklist, please visit: www.greenshill.com

ABOUT THE AUTHOR

Amy Lane exists happily with her noisy family in a crumbling suburban crapmansion, and equally happily with the surprisingly demanding voices who live in her head.

She loves cats, movies, yarn, pretty colors, pretty men, shiny things, and Twu Wuv, and despises housecleaning, low-fat granola bars, and vainglorious prickweenies.

She can be found at her computer, dodging housework, or simultaneously reading, watching television, and knitting, because she likes to freak people out by proving it can be done.

Website: www.greenshill.com
Blog: www.writerslane.blogspot.com
Facebook: Amy Lane Anonymous
Twitter: @amymaclane
Goodreads: goodreads.com/amymaclane

Enjoy this book? Visit RiptidePublishing.com to find more wartime romance!

Unhinge the Universe
ISBN: 978-1-62649-047-5

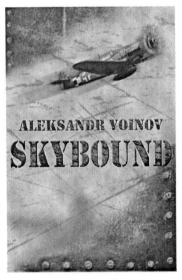

Skybound
ISBN: 978-1-937551-82-7

Earn Bonus Bucks!

Earn 1 Bonus Buck for each dollar you spend. Find out how at RiptidePublishing.com/news/bonus-bucks.

Win Free Ebooks for a Year!

Pre-order coming soon titles directly through our site and you'll receive one entry into a drawing to win free books for a year! Get the details at RiptidePublishing.com/contests.

CPSIA information can be obtained at www.ICGtesting.com
Printed in the USA
LVOW11s1601140615

442423LV00006BA/793/P